"Midnight."

Cindy cried, her heart beating frantically. "It's midnight. I've...I've got to leave. I'm sorry...so sorry."

"Cindy." Thorne reached out for her, but already she was rushing away. He ran a few steps, his pace matching hers. "I'll take you home. Don't worry about missing your ride—"

Tears filled her eyes as she paused to wrap her arms around him, hugging him with all the emotion stored in her heart. "You don't understand."

She was right about that, Thorne mused. She looked stricken—so frightened and so unbelievably unhappy that he longed to ease whatever pain she was suffering.

"It was the most wonderful night of my life. I'll remember it and I'll always...always remember you."

"You won't get a chance to forget me." He tried to keep her with him, but she whirled around and picked up her skirts, racing away as though the very demons of hell were in hot pursuit....

Dear Reader:

The spirit of the Silhouette Romance Homecoming Celebration lives on as each month we bring you six books by continuing stars!

And we have a galaxy of stars planned for 1988. In the coming months, we're publishing romances by many of your favorite authors such as Annette Broadrick, Sondra Stanford and Brittany Young. Beginning in January, Debbie Macomber has written a trilogy designed to cure any midwinter blues. And that's not all—during the summer, Diana Palmer presents her most engaging heros and heroines in a trilogy that will be sure to capture your heart.

Your response to these authors and other authors of Silhouette Romances has served as a touchstone for us, and we're pleased to bring you more books with Silhouette's distinctive medley of charm, wit and—above all—romance.

I hope you enjoy this book and the many stories to come. Come home to romance—for always!

Sincerely,

Tara Hughes
Senior Editor
Silhouette Books

DEBBIE MACOMBER

Cindy and the Prince

Silhouette *Romance*

Published by Silhouette Books New York

America's Publisher of Contemporary Romance

SILHOUETTE BOOKS
300 E. 42nd St., New York, N.Y. 10017

Copyright © 1988 by Debbie Macomber

ISBN: 0-373-08555-9

First Silhouette Books printing January 1988

America's Publisher of Contemporary Romance

Printed in the U.S.A.

Books by Debbie Macomber

DEBBIE MACOMBER

has quickly become one of Silhouette's most prolific authors. As a wife and mother of four, she not only manages to keep her family happy, but she also keeps her publisher and readers happy with each book she writes.

Cindy and the Prince is Book One of Debbie's exciting *Legendary Lovers Trilogy*—three stories based on classic fairy tales. Coming soon from Silhouette Romance are *Some Kind of Wonderful* (Book Two) and *Almost Paradise* (Book Three).

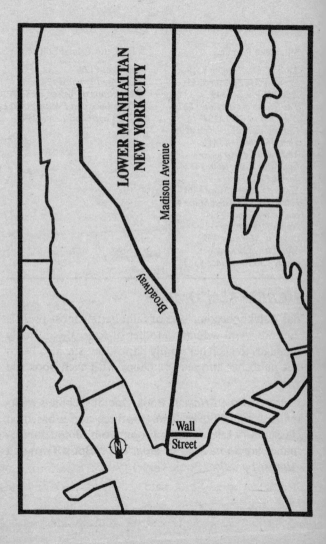

Chapter One

Someday your prince will come," Vanessa Wilbur sang in a strained falsetto voice as she ran a feather duster along the top of the bookcase.

Studiously, Cindy Territo ignored her working partner and vigorously rubbed the thirty-story-view window, removing an imaginary smudge from the thick glass. The pair were janitorial workers for Oakes-Jenning Financial Services and for four nights a week they were responsible for cleaning the executive offices of the company's top officials. Tedious work, but it provided a supplement to Vanessa's family's income so she could pursue her dream of script writing, with high hopes of someday seeing her work performed on Broadway. And the job paid well enough to keep Cindy in computer school.

"You have to admit you spend more time cleaning

Mr. Prince's office than any of the others," Vanessa said, eyeing her friend suspiciously.

Unable to swallow her amusement, Cindy stuffed her cleaning rag into the hip pocket of her coveralls and laughed aloud. "Has anyone told you that you're a hopeless romantic?"

"Of course." Vanessa's eyes shone with unconcealed laughter. She held her feather duster upright, cocked her head to one side and released an exaggerated sigh. "Sometimes I think you, my friend, could be living a modern-day fairy tale."

"A what?" Cindy might be far more cynical than Vanessa, but one of them had to keep her head out of the clouds, she figured.

"A fairy tale."

Cindy did her best to ignore her friend and continued window washing—her least favorite task.

"Someday...some way...a handsome prince will come riding into your life on a white stallion and rescue you from all this."

Abruptly Cindy shook her head. "You've been spending too much time in dreamland again, my friend."

"No, I haven't," Vanessa objected and scooted onto the corner of a large mahogany desk, her short legs swinging. "In fact I believe it's fate. Think about it, girl. Your name is Cindy as in Cinderella and you clean the offices of a man named Prince, as in Prince Charming. Now doesn't that strike you as fate?"

"Thorndike Prince!" Cindy spewed out his name in a burst of laughter.

"And, as I mentioned, you do spend more time in his office than any of the others!"

"He's the first vice president. His office is largest, for heaven's sake."

"But..."

The idea was so ludicrous that Cindy was forced to choke back laughter. "Besides, he's got to be at least sixty...maybe even seventy."

"What makes you think so?"

"First, Oakes-Jenning Financial Services isn't going to make a thirty-three-year-old their first vice president, and second—"

"It's been done before," Vanessa interrupted. Folding her arms, she hopped down from the desk to glare stubbornly at her friend.

"And second of all," Cindy continued undaunted, "I clean his office; I know the man. He's staid, stuffy and sober-minded, and that's just the beginning."

"What do you mean?"

"He's so predictable. He eats the same sandwich—pastrami on rye—nearly every day for lunch and orders it from the same deli. He's so set in his ways that he's as probable as Santa Claus on Christmas Eve. The only thing he knows is business, business, business. Oh, I'm confident that he's dedicated and hardworking, but there's more to life than slaving away in some stuffy office and making oodles of money." A whole lot more—and Cindy sincerely doubted the first vice president knew anything about having fun.

"What do you think about the photograph of the gorgeous brunette that sits on his desk?"

A smile dimpled Cindy's cheeks. "Nothing. I'd venture a guess that Mr. Thorndike Prince has been sedately married to the same woman for fifty years."

"The photo," Vanessa reminded her.

"That's probably the old coot's granddaughter."

"Wrong!"

"Wrong?"

"Yup. How would you like to see a picture of your 'old coot'?"

From the twinkle in Vanessa's dark brown eyes, Cindy knew she was in for a shock. "And just where did you happen to find a picture of ol' Thorndike?"

"In the financial section of this afternoon's paper. Read it and weep, Cindy Territo." She reached inside her cleaning cart and whipped out the folded newspaper, shoving it under Cindy's nose.

One glance at the dark, handsome man in the photograph caused Cindy to suck in a surprised breath. She grabbed the newspaper and held it in both hands as she disbelievingly stared at the picture. "I don't believe it," she murmured in a voice so low it sounded gravelly. "He's, why, he's—"

"Gorgeous," Vanessa supplied with a smile a Cheshire cat would envy.

"Young." The word trembled out from Cindy's dry throat as she had trouble finding her voice. He was gorgeous, all right; she admitted that freely. Rarely had she seen a man more strikingly handsome. He was the type who would stand out in any crowd. Forceful. Persuasive. Vigorous. His face was square and serious, his chin proud and determined. His eyes stared back at her and even from the black-and-white image, Cindy could tell they were an intense gray. There wasn't a hint of amusement in those sharp, keen eyes, and Cindy guessed that the photographer had been lucky to obtain the picture. Perhaps most shocking of all was that Thorndike Prince couldn't be more than thirty-five...if that.

"Well?" Vanessa prodded.

"He isn't exactly the way I pictured him."

"You're right about that," Vanessa said with obvious pleasure. "Now all we need to do is to find a way for the two of you to meet."

"What?" Cindy tore her gaze from the newspaper, confident she'd misunderstood her friend.

"All we need is to come up with a way of getting the two of you together," Vanessa repeated. "You're perfect for each other."

Playfully, Cindy placed the back of her hand against her friend's forehead. "How long have you been running this raging fever?"

"I'm not sick!"

"Maybe not, but you're talking like a crazy woman."

"Come on, Cindy girl, dream a little."

"That's no dream—that's a nightmare." Her hand flew to the barely tamed blond curls sneaking out from beneath the red bandana tied at the back of her head. The blue pinstriped coveralls were reminiscent of a railroad worker's and did nothing to emphasize the feminine curves of her full hips and breasts.

"Naturally you wouldn't look like this."

"I certainly hope not."

"He'd like you, Cindy," Vanessa continued enthusiastically. "I know he would. You're bright and witty, and ol' Thorndike looks like he could use someone to fill his life with love and laughter. I think you may be right about him in that respect. I bet business is all he does think about. And you're so pretty with that naturally blond hair and those baby-blue eyes; the minute he sees you, it'll be like he's been knocked over the head.''

Cindy released a wistful sigh. She didn't need to close her eyes to mentally picture her prince gazing down on her with such a look of tenderness that it stole her breath. Just the thought was enough to produce a warm, tingling sensation in the pit of her stomach.

A frown pinched Vanessa's prominent nose as her gaze grew serious. ''We have one minor problem, though—that woman in the photograph on his desk. I doubt she's his sister. They could be serious.''

'' 'Serious,' '' Cindy repeated before she realized what she was saying. Brusquely she shook her head to shatter the mental image of Thorndike Prince leaning over to kiss her passionately. Within minutes Vanessa had nearly convinced her that at one look, the first vice president of Oakes-Jenning Financial Services would swoon at her feet. How easy it was to dream, but the reality of life faced her every day.

''Come on, Neil Simon, we've got work to do.''

''Neil Simon?''

''You've apparently decided to turn your talent toward writing stage comedies.''

''But, Cindy, I'm serious!''

''I'm not. Someone like Thorndike Prince isn't going to be interested in the cleaning woman who vacuums his office.''

''You're underestimating the man.''

''Enough! I've got work to do even if you don't.''

Although Cindy returned to cleaning and scrubbing with a vigor that had been lacking earlier, her thoughts were far from the tasks at hand. Even when she left the

Financial Center for the dark, windy streets of Manhattan, her thoughts centered on the tall, dark man in the photograph. It wasn't like her to be so affected by a man simply because he was good-looking. But Thorndike Prince was far more than handsome; something deep within her had instantly responded to him, had innocently, naively reached out to him. She saw in him the elusive qualities she'd been searching for in a man for the past twenty-two years. He was proud yet honest. Shrewd yet gentle. Demanding yet patient.

The December wind whistled down the canyon of tall office buildings and Cindy tucked the thick wool coat more snugly around her, burying her hands deep in her pockets. A quick glance at the clock in front of the jeweler's across the street told her Uncle Sal would be there any minute. No sooner had the thought formed when the sleek black limousine eased to a stop against the curb. The front door swung open as Cindy approached and she quickly climbed inside, savoring the warmth.

"You been waiting long?"

"Only a couple of minutes." Cindy gave her uncle a reassuring smile.

He removed the black driver's cap and unbuttoned the crisp chauffeur's uniform, letting out a deep breath. "Remind me to talk to your aunt. The cleaners must have shrunk this jacket."

"Right," Cindy said, swallowing a laugh. More than likely it was Aunt Theresa's cooking that was responsible for the tight jacket, but she wasn't about to tell her uncle that.

As the limousine wove through the New York traffic, Cindy stared out the window, more tired than she could remember.

"You're quiet tonight," her uncle commented thoughtfully.

"I'd think you'd count your blessings." Life in a large Italian family rarely left a moment's peace. Sal and Theresa's home was the hub of the Territo clan. Her aunt and uncle had raised Cindy as their own, loving her, nurturing her with all the warmth they gave their natural child. Cindy's own parents had divorced when she was too young to remember, and her mother had died when Cindy was five. She'd never heard from her father, and when she'd started grade school she'd taken the name Territo to avoid confusion.

Sal chuckled. "Maybe I should be grateful for the quiet. When I left the house this afternoon your aunt was blistering the sidewalk with her rantings."

"What happened now?"

"She found Tony and Maria necking on the fire escape again."

At fifteen, Cindy's cousin was already showing the potential for breaking many a young girl's heart. "That Tony's too hot-blooded."

Sal chuckled, sent a proud glance to his niece and playfully nudged her with his elbow. "He's too much like his old man, huh?"

"Right. He probably doesn't even feel the cold."

The car grew silent again, and once more Cindy felt her uncle's eyes on her. "You feeling okay?"

"I'm just tired."

"How many more weeks you got of school?"

"A couple." Two full weeks and then she could rest and concentrate on the fast-approaching Christmas holidays. Christmas was sneaking up on her this year. Although she had set aside the money from her last paycheck, she hadn't even started her shopping. There hadn't been time and wouldn't be until her computer classes were dismissed for the winter quarter.

Her uncle parked the limousine in front of the apartment building in a space reserved for him. Nothing was posted to claim this curb for Sal's limousine, but the neighborhood, out of love and respect, made sure there was room for him to park each night.

The apartment was quiet. Cindy and her uncle paused in the crowded entryway to remove their coats. Cindy hung hers on the brass coatrack while her uncle reverently placed his jacket inside the hall closet. His cap was tucked in place on the shelf above the rack.

"You hungry?" her uncle whispered.

"Not tonight." Aunt Theresa kept a large plate of food warming in the oven for them and her uncle and Cindy often sat in front of Johnny Carson and enjoyed their late-night dinner.

"You sure you're feeling okay?" Sal squinted his eyes as he studied her carefully.

"I'm fine. I think I'll take a hot bath and go to bed."

"You do that." Already her uncle was heading for the kitchen, eager for his meal.

Cindy's bedroom was tiny, as were all the bedrooms in the apartment. There was hardly room to walk between the double bed and the heavy mahogany dresser that had been her mother's as a child. The closet was little more than an indentation in the wall. A faded curtain hung in front of it, serving as the door. Cindy glanced around the room with fresh eyes. Thorndike Prince definitely wouldn't be interested in a woman who slept in a room such as this. Her thoughts drifted to the dark woman in the photograph on his desk. No doubt her bedroom was carpeted with lush Oriental rugs and decorated with a fancy brass bedroom set. Perhaps there was even a fireplace.... Cindy sighed and sat on the corner of her mattress feeling the hopelessness of it all. Vanessa had told her it was time to dream a little, and that was exactly what Cindy planned to do: she was going to save this special feeling she had for Thorndike Prince for her dreams.

After luxuriating in a tub filled with hot soapy water, Cindy fell into a deep, natural sleep.

The following day she even managed not to think about Vanessa's crazy schemes throughout her classes. Nor did she allow thoughts of her prince to invade her mind while she hurried home from school and changed into her work clothes. However, the minute she stepped into the Oakes-Jenning Financial Services building, Cindy was assaulted on all sides by dreams she had no right to entertain.

"Hi," Vanessa grumbled as she checked the supplies on her cleaning cart.

"What's wrong with you?" Of the pair, Vanessa was usually the one with the ready smile and quick conversation.

"Traffic was a nightmare."

"Hey, girl, this is New York. What do you expect?"

"A little sympathy would come in handy."

"Poor, Vanessa...poor, poor Vanessa." Soothingly, Cindy stroked her friend's arm. "Did that help?"

"A little," she grumbled and led the way to the service elevator. They rode it to the main floor, then transferred to the passenger one. Bob Knight, the security officer who guarded the front entrance, waved as they continued through the front foyer.

Cindy leaned her weight against the back of the elevator as the heavy door glided silently shut. Already she was concerned about cleaning Thorndike's office. The room would never be the same to her again. She couldn't just empty his garbage without wondering what was happening in his life and knowing she could never be a part of it.

"Hey, did you see that?" Vanessa cried excitedly, making a futile attempt to stop the elevator.

"See what?" Cindy was instantly alert.

The moment the elevator hit the thirtieth floor, Vanessa pushed the button that sent them backtracking in a rushing movement.

"Vanessa, what's going on?"

"Give me a minute and I'll tell you."

"Tell me what?" Cindy chuckled at the way her friend anxiously bit her bottom lip. "No doubt you've witnessed the living answer to life's difficulties? Perhaps you've discovered the secret to peace and goodwill for all mankind?"

The instant the doors glided open Vanessa grabbed Cindy's arm and jerked her out of the elevator. "Look at this," she cried, slapping her friend across the back as she shoved her in front of a large notice board.

"Look at what?" The only thing she could see was information about some type of party.

"Read it out loud," Vanessa instructed with tattered patience.

Shrugging her shoulders, Cindy complied. "The Oakes-Jenning Christmas Ball, 7:30 p.m., December 15. Hotel St. Moritz, Grand Ballroom. By invitation only."

"Well?" Vanessa's eyebrows arched with devilish humor.

"Well, what?" Gradually a dawning light seeped into Cindy's perplexed brain. "You're nuts! You couldn't possibly mean for me to..."

"It's the perfect way to get you two together."

"But..." So many excuses crowded Cindy's mind that she couldn't say them all. The first one to untwist itself from the tip of her tongue was the most obvious. "I don't have an invitation."

"Hey, there are ways—"

"Forget it!" Cindy hoped she'd said it in a way that would cancel all further arguments. She stepped back into the elevator and waited for Vanessa to join her.

"I'm not going to forget it and neither are you. It's fate...Kismet. I knew it the minute I saw Thorndike Prince's picture in the newspaper and so did you, so don't try to argue with me."

"I'm not arguing," Cindy replied calmly. "I simply refuse to discuss it."

"But why?"

Faking a yawn, Cindy cupped her hand over her mouth and idly glanced at her watch.

"All right, all right, I get the message," Vanessa grumbled under her breath. "But you aren't kidding me one bit. You're dying to attend that Christmas Ball."

Was she? Cindy asked herself as the night progressed. Dusting Mr. Prince's outer office granted her the solitude to think about the magic of a Christmas ball, and she quickly realized her friend was right once again. Cindy had never thought of herself as being so transparent, but she would gladly have sacrificed herself to the taunts of three ugly stepsisters for the opportunity to attend such a gala event. Only she didn't have any stepsisters and she wasn't Cinderella. But a ball...the Christmas Ball...Nowhere else would she have the opportunity to introduce herself to her prince and be accepted as his equal but in a place as enchanting as a Christmas ball. Perhaps Vanessa was fey....

Naw, Cindy discounted that thought. Her working partner simply possessed a wildly romantic heart. But then, so did charwoman Cindy.

Her feather duster ran across Thorndike Prince's secretary's desk and for the first time since she'd been hired by the janitorial department, Cindy wondered about the woman who spent so much of her day with Thorndike Prince. Mrs. Hillard rarely let anything go to waste. Even discarded pages of stationery were neatly trimmed into scratch pads, stapled together at the top corners. The woman's theme appeared to be Waste Not, Want Not.

Cindy spent only a bare minimum of time in Mr. Prince's office. Other than a dusting now and again and an occasional vacuuming, the room was surprisingly neat, which was something she couldn't say about the other executives' quarters. As she emptied his garbage, a smile touched her deep blue eyes to note the name The Deli Belly, the delicatessen from which Thorndike ordered his lunch. He was apparently a creature of habit, but then they all were, weren't they?

As Cindy moved from one office to the next she did her utmost to contain her thoughts, but her mind turned traitor, and the image of the crystal ball dangling from the center of the ballroom and the crowded room full of dancing couples kept flitting into her mind. In every image, Cindy and her prince were in the center of the Grand Ballroom, arms entwined around each other.

"Well?" Vanessa said, startling Cindy.

She recovered with astonishing dexterity. "Well, what?"

"Have you been thinking about the ball, Cinderella?"

"It's not going to work." It was a measure of her fascination with Thorndike Prince to admit she'd given the matter a second thought. It was an impossible scheme from beginning to end.

"It'll work," Vanessa said with blind optimism.

"Then where's my fairy godmother?"

With a saucy grin, Vanessa polished her nails against the yoke of her cotton shirt. "Hey, sweetie, you're looking at her."

"And my coach led by two perfectly matched white stallions. And how about turning mice into footmen? Is that trick up your sleeve as well?"

For a moment Vanessa looked concerned, then she smiled and flexed her fingers. "I'm working on those. There's no need to worry."

"Are you working on a floor-length chiffon gown at the same time?"

"Sure..."

"If I were a fairy godmother, I'd tackle the invitation business right away."

"Right." For the first time Vanessa looked daunted. "I didn't realize this was going to be such a headache."

"And that's only the beginning."

"I don't think I want to hear it all."

Cindy turned back to her cart, pushing it down the wide hallway, humming as she went. It was nice to dream, but that was all it could ever be for her and the prince: a fanciful dream.

Almost by rote, Cindy picked up the green metal garbage can of the secretary to the third vice president and dumped its contents into the large plastic bag on the end of her cart. As she did so a flash of gold caught her eye. Out of curiosity, she reached for it, and when she read the gilt printing, her heart rushed to her throat, nearly choking off her breath.

Holding the paper in both hands, she walked out of the room in a daze. "Vanessa!" she cried. "Vanessa, hurry. I don't believe it.... I think I'm living through an episode of *Twilight Zone.*"

Her partner met her in the hallway. "What is it?"

"Look." Reverently, she handed the folded piece of paper to her friend.

"It's an invitation to the ball," Vanessa whispered, raising her round, shocked eyes to meet Cindy's. "I don't believe it!" Then her dark eyes brightened as she waved an imaginary wand over Cindy's head. "Did you feel the fairy dust?"

"It's coming down like rain, my friend," Cindy cried shaking her head with awe and wonder.

"Where did you find it?"

"In the garbage."

"You've got to be kidding!"

Cindy shook her head. "They must have been mailed out last week sometime."

"And apparently Miss Reynolds has decided not to attend, in which case you will humbly accept on her behalf."

"But—"

"It's fate! Surely you're not going to argue with me now!"

"No." Cindy was more than willing to accept this unexpected gift. She'd attend this ball and satisfy her inquisitiveness regarding Thorndike Prince. She'd indulge herself this one time and only this once.

On the evening of December 15, Cindy's stomach was a mass of nerves. A beehive would have held less rumbling activity. Her cousin, Tony, knocked on her bedroom door and called, "Vanessa's here."

"Okay, tell her I'll be right out." Squaring her shoulders, Cindy forced herself to smile and walked into the living room, where her family and Vanessa were impatiently waiting.

Her friend stood as Cindy entered the room. "Oh, Cindy, you're . . . beautiful."

Cindy's aunt dabbed the corner of one eye and murmured something in Italian. "She looks just like her mother."

Vanessa didn't seem to hear her. "Where did you ever find such an elegant gown?" The sweetheart neckline was trimmed with the finest lace and was worn off the shoulders. The bodice fit snugly against her torso and the waistline was slightly raised. The skirt was made up of layer upon layer of pale blue chiffon that formed wide-tiered ruffles.

"Do you like it?" Slowly she whirled around, letting Vanessa view the full effect.

"I'm speechless."

For Vanessa, that was saying something. Cindy's gaze rested lovingly on her aunt.

Aunt Theresa lifted her hand in mock salute. "It was nothing... an early Christmas gift."

"She made it?" Vanessa gasped.

"A dress is not made," Theresa chided mockingly. "It is sewn with loving fingers."

"Where'd you get the purse?"

Cindy lifted the small pearl-beaded clutch. "My Aunt Sofia."

"And the combs?"

Cindy's hands flew to her hair, swirled upon her head and held in place by pearl combs. "Those were my mother's."

"You look more like a princess than anyone I've ever seen. I don't know what to say."

"For once," Cindy laughed.

Vanessa walked circles around her a couple of times, shaking her head in wonder.

"How are you getting there?"

"My uncle's dropping me off and picking me up later."

"Excellent plan."

"Listen." Suddenly Cindy's nerve abandoned her. She was living her dream just as she'd always wanted, but something deep inside her was screaming that she was playing the part of a fool—a romantic fool, but a fool nonetheless. "I'm not sure I'm doing the right thing. Sheila will probably be there." On close examination of the brunette in the photograph on Thorndike's desk, Cindy and Vanessa had seen the other woman's bold signature across the bottom of the picture.

"She might," Vanessa agreed. "But you'll do fine." For good measure she added another imaginary sparkling of fairy dust. "The enchantment is set, so don't worry."

"What? Me worry?" Cindy said, crossing her eyes and twisting her face like her favorite madcap character.

Everyone laughed, nearly drowning out the sound of the honk from the limousine in the street below.

"You ready?" Aunt Theresa asked, draping a warm shawl around Cindy's shoulders.

"As ready as I'll ever be," she said, expelling a deep breath.

Her Uncle Sal was standing outside the limousine, holding open the back door for her. "You ready, Miss?" he asked in a dignified voice that nearly dissolved Cindy into giggles.

She climbed into the back and realized that of all the nights she'd ridden with her uncle, this was the first time she'd ever been seated in back. "Hey, this is nice," she called forward, running her hands along the smooth velvet cushion, astonished at all the space.

"We have one problem," her uncle informed her, meeting her gaze in the rearview mirror.

"What's that?"

"I'm sorry, kiddo, but I've got to have the limo to pick up the Buckhardt party before one."

"That won't be any problem," Cindy returned cheerfully. "Cinderella is supposed to leave the ball before midnight anyway."

Chapter Two

Bored, Thorne Prince stood in the farthest corner of the ballroom, with a look of studied indifference on his face. He idly held a glass of champagne. He hated these sort of functions; they were a waste of his valuable time. He'd been obligated to attend this silly Christmas party, but he held out little hope of enjoying it. To complicate matters, Sheila couldn't attend with him. She, at least, would have made the evening tolerable. Hoping he wasn't being obvious, Thorne glanced at his gold wristwatch and wondered if anyone would notice if he silently slipped away.

"Prince, old boy, good to see you." Rutherford Hayden stepped to his side and slapped him hard across the back.

Thorne's response was a grim smile. He had no use for the man who was looking to further himself in the company by ingratiating himself with Thorne by means other than job skills and performance.

"Fine party."

"Yes." If the man hoped to engage Thorne in long-winded conversation, he was going to be disappointed.

A moment of awkward silence passed during which Thorne did nothing to ease the tension. Rutherford paused and cleared his throat. "I've been giving some thought to your suggestion regarding the Hughes account, and I—"

"It was an order, not a suggestion." The hard line of Thorne's mouth remained inflexible. Damn! Hayden was going to trap him into talking business, and he'd be stuck with this inept bore half the night. To refuse would only heighten the already growing dislike between them. In spite of his incompetence, Hayden had the ear of Paul Jenning, the company president. Apparently the two had been high-school chums and on occasion played golf together.

"I'm back," Cindy said, feigning breathlessness as she sauntered up to Thorne's side. She gazed at him with wide, adoring eyes. "Thank you for holding my champagne." She took the glass from his lifeless hand and turned her attention to Hayden. "It's good to see you again, Ruffie." Deliberately she used the nickname she knew he disliked. A woman didn't empty a man's wastepaper basket for a year without learning something about him. Cindy was a silent witness to the habits, likes and dislikes of all the occupants of the executive offices.

Rutherford Hayden glanced from Cindy to Thorne, then back to her again. "I'm afraid I don't recall the pleasure."

"Cindy," she informed him and offered him her hand. He politely shook it, and Cindy fluttered her lashes for the full, dazzling effect.

"'Ruffie'?" Thorne asked, cocking one eyebrow, mocking amusement evident in his voice.

"Yes, well..." Rutherford looked into the dancing couples that occupied the extensive ballroom floor. "I won't keep you any longer. We can discuss this Hughes matter another time."

"Good idea." Thorne knew from the way Hayden's eyes were scanning the crowd that he would move on to easier prey.

"Nice seeing you again, Tami."

"Cindy," she corrected, taking a sip of the champagne. The bubbly liquid slid down the back of her throat, and she smiled beguilingly up at the irritating man.

As soon as Hayden was out of earshot, Cindy turned and handed the glass back to Thorne.

"Now," she said, her eyes twinkling. "I won't disturb you any longer," she murmured sweetly. "You can get back to your pouting. But you really shouldn't brood, you know—age lines."

Thorne's mouth sagged open with complete astonishment. "'Pout—ing'?"

"It's true," she said without so much as blinking. "You're a sad disappointment to me, Thorndike Prince."

Thorne hadn't the foggiest notion who this chit was, but he gave her points for originality. "I'm devastated to hear it."

"I don't doubt it." If he didn't possess the common sense to recognize her as his Cinderella, then there was little she could do about it.

"Just who are you?"

"If you don't know yet, then we're in worse shape than I thought."

"Cindy who?" He studied her closely and couldn't recall ever meeting her.

"If you had a lick of sense, you'd recognize me."

"We've met?"

"Sort of..." Cindy hedged, her nerve flagging. "All right, since you're obviously not the prince I thought, I guess it won't do any harm to tell you. I'm Cinderella, but unfortunately, you're not my prince—you're much too cynical."

"Cinderella?" Thorne felt laughter expand his chest and would have let it escape if she'd shown the least bit of amusement, but she was dead serious.

"You needn't worry," Cindy said. "I won't trouble you any longer. You can go back to your brooding." With that, she sashayed away, leaving him without so much as glancing over her shoulder.

Pouting! Brooding! Of all the nerve! No one spoke to him like that! A Prince neither pouted nor brooded!

Gradually the anger wore away and a hint of a smile wooed the edges of his mouth. Before he knew what was happening, Thorne grinned. The amusement swelled within him and he forced back the desire to laugh outright. He didn't recall that the Cinderella of old had this much grit. This one did—rare grit—and

almost against his will he sought her out in the crowded
room. He found her standing against the wall opposite his own. Willingly her eyes met his, and she raised
her champagne glass in a silent toast. Her eyes were a
brilliant, bottomless shade of vibrant blue, and even
from this distance he could see them sparkling at him.
Alluring. That was the word that flashed into Thorne's
mind. She was the most utterly appealing woman he'd
seen in ages.

From the way her eyes held his, he saw she was interested and interesting. It wasn't unusual for a woman
to approach him; he was intelligent enough to know he
was considered a "good catch," and many a debu-
tante would like to sink her eyeteeth into him. He knew
that in time this woman, too, would return to his side
to strike up another conversation. He'd play this one
cool, but given the right incentive he'd forgive her for
insulting his pride. Although—damn it all—she was
right; he had been pouting. But brooding—now that
was going too far.

For her part, Cindy was acutely disappointed in
Thorndike Prince. He was everything she'd expected
and nothing like she'd hoped. A contradiction in terms,
she realized, but she could find no other way to describe her feelings. He was so cynical—as though the
beauty of this lovely evening and the Christmas sea-
son left him untouched. For hours she'd been studying him. At first she'd been captivated, enticed. Only
later did her fascination begin to dim. Whimsically,
she'd built him up in her mind, and he'd fallen far
short of her expectations. He was her knight in shin-
ing armor. Her hero. The man of her dreams. She'd

imagined him gallant and exciting and had found him bored and cynical. Twice he'd glanced at his watch and once...once, he'd even had the audacity to *yawn*. Life appeared to be so predictable and mundane to Thorndike Prince that the beauty that surrounded him did little to faze him.

Cindy was disappointed, but she refused to waste this precious evening. She'd made her pitch and announced who she was. Mission accomplished. She was convinced she'd best forget about her prince, but there wasn't any reason to waste this night. Cindy intended to have a marvelous time and not surprisingly she did just that as she mingled with the guests, placing names with faces. Feeling a bit smug because she knew their secrets and they knew nothing of her, she danced, nibbled on the hors d'oeuvres and tapped the toe of her high-heeled shoe to the lighthearted beat of the orchestra music.

An hour. Thorne had been waiting an hour for the mysterious Cinderella to return and she'd ostentatiously remained on the other side of the ballroom. Except for the silent toast she'd given him earlier, she'd granted him little more than a disinterested glance now and again. Once, she'd danced with Barney, a young executive, and Thorne had been hard-pressed not to cross the room and inform her that James Barney was no prince! But the thought of taking such an action was so utterly irrational that Thorne had been stunned ever to have entertained it.

Another time, the sound of her laughter had drifted over to him, and Thorne thought he couldn't remember ever hearing anything more musical. She intrigued him. He discovered he couldn't stop watching her. An unreasonable anger began to build inside him when she danced with two other men.

Finally when he could tolerate it no longer, Thorne reached for another glass of champagne and marched across the room.

"I think you'd best explain yourself," he said without preamble.

At first Cindy was too stunned to speak. "I beg your pardon."

"I'll have you know, I never brood." Her blue eyes fairly gleamed like liquid sapphire as a smile brought her mouth into the most sensuous movement he'd ever witnessed. "And this business about being Cinderella—now that's going a bit overboard, don't you think?"

"No, but please call me Cindy. Cinderella is such an outdated name."

She laughed then, that sweet, musical laugh that had fascinated him earlier. He stared at her, unable to look away. She reminded him of snowflakes and kittens, innocence and youth. It took all his restraint not to reach out and pull her into his arms. Good Lord, he hadn't drunk that much champagne. "Would you care to dance?" he found himself asking.

She nodded eagerly, and Thorne escorted her onto the floor, his hand guiding her at the small of her back. When they reached the outer fringes of the dance floor, Thorne turned her into his embrace. In the beginning he held her at arm's length, almost afraid of what would happen to him if he brought her soft feminine body against his own. Maybe she'd disappear, vanish into thin air. He half expected to wake up from this

trance and find the entire company staring at him while
he swirled around the room all alone.

Although Thorne held up the pretense of dancing, all
of his concentration was focused on merely looking at
his intriguing partner. On closer inspection he found
her to be truly lovely; she was more than pretty, she was
breathtakingly beautiful. Innocent yet enticing. Doc-
ile yet challenging. Her skin looked as soft as satin and
felt as warm as a spring day. He didn't dare think about
what that marvelous little mouth would taste like. He
resisted the instinct to bring her into the circle of his
arms, although their movements were awkward and
strangely out of sync.

Finally Cindy shook her head, stopped dancing and
dropped her arms. Her gaze found his, her disappointment keen. In the space of a few hours, her prince
had managed to shatter every illusion she dared to form
about him. "Not only are you a terrible disappointment to me, but you can't dance worth a darn, either."
Disgusted, she stared at him, defying him to disagree
with her.

Thorne didn't—she was right. Without saying a
word, he brought her back into his arms, only this time
he held her the way he'd wanted to from the first,
pressing her body intimately to his. Her full breasts
brushed against his torso. Thigh aligned to thigh. No
more games, no more secrets.

Cindy slipped her arms around his neck and lay her
head along the chiseled line of his jaw. The music was
a favorite Christmas melody, and her eyes drifted shut
as she wrapped herself in the enchantment of the song.

They moved as one, as though they had spent a lifetime practicing together for this one night. A woman

had never felt more right in Thorne's arms. A man had never seemed more in command as he led Cindy from one end of the dance floor to the other without missing a step, guiding, leading, dictating every action.

"Do you always hum along with the music?" Thorne asked unexpectedly.

Cindy's eyes flew open and she nearly stumbled over his feet as her step faltered. "I'm sorry... I didn't realize."

"No problem," Thorne murmured, chuckling; he cradled the back of her head and guided her temple to its former position against his jaw. After she'd called him a cynic, a brooding one to boot, he felt he owed her a bit of honesty as well. "You were only slightly off-key."

Cindy could feel him smile and she relaxed, not wanting to do anything to disturb the wonder of the moment.

Maybe she'd been wrong. Maybe, just maybe, he could be her prince after all. Thorne was holding her just as she'd dreamed and from the way his arms tightened around her at the end of the song, it felt as though he never intended to let her go.

"Would it be selfish to request another dance?"

"Cinderella's prince did," Cindy whispered, her heart tripping with a glorious melody that had nothing to do with the orchestra's music.

"Then I should, don't you think?"

It was all Cindy could do to nod. They danced again and again and again, neither speaking, each savoring the simple pleasure of being held. The only thought in Thorne's mind was the woman in his arms.

The only thought in Cindy's mind was that fairy tales can come true; she was living one.

"You say I'm a disappointment to you?" he ventured at the end of the dance. He couldn't hold her any longer without trying to discover everything he could about her.

Cindy lifted her head and gazed at him. "Not anymore."

Thorne felt the full dazzling impact of her blue eyes on him. "Not anymore?" he repeated, smiling despite his effort not to. "Have we met before?" He was sure they hadn't; he wouldn't have forgotten her or those incredible blue eyes, but one look and she'd seen straight through him.

"Never," she confirmed.

"But you know me?"

Cindy dropped her gaze. "Yes and no."

"You *are* an employee of Oakes-Jenning?"

"Yes." Amusement slashed her soft mouth until the corners quivered with the effort to hold back a smile. "Did you think I'd crashed your precious party?" That was so close to the truth that she quickly averted her gaze.

Thorne ignored her obvious enjoyment of this one-sided conversation. "How did you know Rutherford Hayden's nickname is Ruffie?"

"The same way I know you hate tuna salad." Cindy's gaze fell upon the rows and rows of tables loaded with a spectacular menu of salads, meats and cheeses. "Now, if you'll excuse me, I'd like to get something to eat."

He took a step forward in an effort to stop her. "No."

"No?"

Thorne realized he must sound like an idiot, but he didn't want to let her go. "Would you mind if I joined you?"

"Not at all," she said, her heart leaping for joy once again.

"My mother sent you, didn't she?" Thorne breathed a sigh of relief; he had it all figured out. His mother had been after him for years to give her grandchildren. She must have hunted for months to find someone as perfect as Cindy.

"Your mother? No."

The honesty in her eyes couldn't be doubted. But even if his mother had put Cindy up to this, it didn't explain the instant, overwhelming attraction he felt for her.

Bemused, Thorne followed her through the long line that had formed at the buffet tables, heaping his plate with a wide variety of the offerings.

"What? No pastrami?" Cindy teased after they'd found a table in the crowded room.

Thorne paused, his napkin only half unfolded. His eyes cut through her. "I had a pastrami sandwich for lunch. You couldn't have known that, could you?"

"No. It was an educated guess." Cindy focused her attention on buttering her dinner roll.

"An educated guess? Like my not liking tuna?"

"No." Deliberately she took a bite of her seafood salad, tasting shrimp, crab and another delicacy she couldn't name.

Patiently Thorne waited until she had finished chewing. "But you know me?"

"A little." Not nearly as well as she wanted to.

"How?"

"I *do* work for Oakes-Jenning," she said and glanced at the huge green olives he'd removed from the top of the dainty sandwiches. "Are you going to eat those?"

Thorne's gaze followed her own to his plate. "The green olives—good grief, no."

"Can I have them?"

Without ceremony, Thorne delivered three to her plate, then fastidiously wiped his hands clean on the linen napkin.

Eagerly Cindy picked up an olive and placed it between her lips, luxuriously sucking out the pimento, then popping the entire thing in her mouth. When she'd finished, she paused to lick the tips of her fingers free of juice. Thorne's scowl stopped her when she reached for another. The lines at the side of his mouth had deepened, and she noted the vein pulsing in his temple. Alarm filled her. Her worst fear had been realized: unwittingly, she'd committed some terrible faux pas.

"What did I do wrong?" she asked in a fear-laced whisper. She dropped her hands to her lap and clenched the napkin, watching him expectantly.

For a long moment, their eyes locked and held. Thorne had been mesmerized, watching her eat the olive. Such a simple pleasure, and she'd made it appear highly sensuous. He couldn't seem to take his eyes off her—or off the tempting shape of her mouth. Again he felt the overwhelming urge to kiss her and experience for himself the sweetness of her lips. Her eyes, her mouth, the curve of her cheek. Everything about her completely and utterly captivated him. For years women had used their bodies and their wits in a effort to entice him. But no woman had ever had the effect on him that this one did with the simple act of eating an olive.

"What did you do wrong?" Thorne repeated, shaking his head to clear his befuddled thoughts. "What makes you think you did anything wrong?"

"You were looking at me...funny."

He smiled then, forcing the edges of his mouth to curve upward. "Then I apologize."

Cindy relaxed and reached for the second olive. Thorne's gaze widened and he groaned inwardly, setting his fork beside his plate.

The music started up again long before they'd finished their meal and unconsciously Cindy tapped her toe to the beat. Christmas was her favorite time of year, and the orchestra seemed to know all the carols she loved best.

"Would you like to dance again?" Thorne asked.

Cindy nodded. She wouldn't refuse the opportunity to be in her prince's arms. This was her night, a night for enchantment, and she wanted to remember and relive every moment of it for the rest of her life. Tomorrow she would go back to being plain, simple Cindy, the girl who cleaned his office. But tonight...tonight she was the alluring woman he longed to hold in his arms.

By unspoken agreement they stood together and walked to the center of the dance floor. Thorne turned Cindy into his arms, holding her close, savoring the feel of her, that special scent that was only hers, and the warmth of her nearness. He felt as if he were a hundred years old in ways she knew nothing about and, conversely, that he'd just turned twenty-one all over again. She did this to him and he hadn't an inkling why.

Thorne's arms tightened around her, anchoring her against him. Both his hands were around her waist and he laid his cheek along hers and closed his eyes. To think that only a few hours earlier he'd been contemplating sneaking away from this party, having found it a deadly bore. Now he dreaded the time it would end, praying that each minute would stretch out so that nothing would destroy this night and his time with this woman.

Cindy pressed her cheek to his and prayed she'd always remember every minute of this night. She planned to store each detail in her heart. She couldn't possibly hope to explain it to anyone; mere words were inadequate to describe the warm feeling she shared with Thorne. This magical, mystical night was hers and hers alone. She would have a lifetime to treasure these precious hours and relive each minute over and over in her mind.

Even when the music became lively, Thorne held her as though it were the slowest dance of the night. He wanted to kiss her so badly that he was forced to inhale sharp, even breaths several times to restrain his desire. Thorndike Prince did not make a spectacle of himself on the dance floor for any reason. However he soon discovered that the temptation was too strong. Her nearness was more than any sane man could resist and he turned his head ever so slightly and ran his mouth over her ear.

Cindy released a sigh of pleasure and moved her hands to the back of Thorne's neck, running her finger through the thick dark hair. When his lips sought the hollow of her throat, she groaned his name in a low, aching sigh.

Unexpectedly Thorne dropped his arms and reached for her hand. "Let's get out of here," he said in a voice that sounded strangely unlike his own.

He led her off the ballroom floor as though he couldn't leave fast enough. "Did you bring a coat?"

"A shawl."

Irritably he held out his hand, palm upward. "Give me your ticket."

Her fingers shook as she opened the beaded clutch and retrieved the small tab. "Where . . . where are you going?"

He sounded almost angry, certainly impatient. "Anywhere but here," he mumbled.

He left her then and Cindy stood alone, pondering the strangeness of his actions. She wanted to ask him more, longed to know why he looked as though he wanted to rip her limb from limb. But when he returned she said nothing, silently following him as he led her out of the ballroom and into the hallway to the elevator.

A male voice called out to them. "Thorne, you're not leaving, are you?"

Cindy twisted her head around at the unexpected sound of the voice, but Thorne applied pressure to her back, directing her forward.

"That man was talking to you."

"I have no desire to talk to anyone," he said stiffly, escorting her into the crowded elevator. They stepped off at the ground floor and Thorne led her to the entrance of the hotel.

The doorman stepped forward and asked. "Taxi, sir?"

Thorne looked at the man as though he hadn't heard him. He decided quickly, glancing at Cindy. "No." He grabbed her hand then, and guided her across the busy street to the paved pathway that led to the interior of Central Park.

"Thorne," Cindy whispered, uncertain. "Why are you so angry?"

"Angry?" He paused in front of the large fish pond.

The moon beamed golden rays all around them, and Cindy could see that his face was intent, his mouth bracketed with harsh lines. His gray eyes were narrowed and hard, yet when they rested on her she saw them soften.

"I'm not angry," he said at last, his breathing labored. "I'm..." He paused and rammed his hands into his pants pockets. "I don't know what I am. You're right, I am angry, but not at you."

"Then who?"

He shook his head and his eyes grew warm and lambent as he studied her upturned face. Almost as though he didn't know what he was doing, Thorne pulled his hands from his pockets and cupped her face, staring at her with a thoroughness that brought a heated rush of color to her cheeks. "You're so beautiful," he whispered with a reverence that shook his voice.

Cindy dropped her eyes.

His grip tightened almost imperceptibly. "It's true," he continued. "I've never known anyone as lovely."

"Why did you bring me here?"

Thorne expelled his breath in a low rush, and his words were an odd mixture of anger and wonder. "For the most selfish of reasons. I wanted to kiss you."

Cindy's questioning gaze sought his. "Then why haven't you? Cinderella's waiting."

He smiled then. "You're taking this prince stuff seriously, aren't you?"

"Very."

He ran his thumb across her bottom lip and his eyes grew serious. "I've never experienced anything like this."

"Me either." It was important that he know this phenomenon was as much a shock to her. She hadn't expected anything like this to happen, hadn't believed it ever would. When she'd first seen him, her disappointment had been acute and profound. But all that had changed the moment he'd come to her and asked her to dance. From that time forward he had magically been transformed into the prince who'd dominated her dreams for weeks. He was everything she'd imagined and a thousand things more.

"I haven't any right," he said, but his mouth inched closer to hers as though he wanted her to stop him.

She couldn't—not when she longed for his kiss the way she did; not when every cell of her being was crying out for the taste of his mouth over hers.

The ragged beat of his heart echoed her own as Cindy flattened her hands against his chest and slowly, deliberately, tilted her face to receive his kiss. They were so close their breath mingled. Cindy parted her lips, eager now. She stood on tiptoe as Thorne gently lowered his lips onto hers. His mouth was firm and so unbelievably tender that Cindy felt a tear form at the corner of her eye. Their mouths clung, and Cindy's hands crept upward to meet behind his neck.

"Oh, Lord—so sweet, so very sweet," Thorne groaned and buried his face in the milky-smooth slope of her neck. "I knew it would be like this. I knew it would be this sweet." His breathing was ragged, uneven.

Cindy felt as though she'd been shocked, stunned into speechlessness. Her whole body went numb, tingling with wonder. As difficult as it was, she resisted the urge to place her fingers to her lips to test the sensation. Thorne looked equally shaken. They broke apart and Cindy teetered for a moment until she found her balance.

Their eyes met and held for a timeless second. When Thorne reached for her, Cindy walked willingly into his arms, as though it were the only place in all creation where she truly belonged. His mouth was eager, hungry upon hers, twisting, turning, tasting, testing as though he had to reexperience these sensations and hadn't believed this wonderful feeling could be real.

When he released her, Cindy was weak and trembling. She looked up at Thorne and noted he was unnaturally pale.

Without questioning her, Thorne took a step back and removed his heavy overcoat. Gently, he placed it over her shoulders. "You're cold," he whispered. His hands lingered on her shoulders, and it looked as though he had to restrain himself from kissing her again.

"No," she murmured, shaking her head. "It's not the cold. It's you—you make me tremble."

"Look what you do to me." He captured her hand and placed it over his pounding heart. A frown drove his dark brows together. "I'm no schoolboy. What's happening to us?"

Cindy smiled and pressed a gentle kiss to the corner of his mouth. "Magic, I think."

"Black magic?" He regarded her suspiciously, but his eyes were smiling.

"No, this is the very best kind."

He agreed. Nothing that felt this good, this wonderful, could ever be wrong. He placed his arm around her shoulder and led her to one of the many benches that faced the huge fish pond.

Silently they sat together, neither speaking, neither needing words. Thorne continued to hold her simply because releasing her was unthinkable. His mind whirled with a hundred questions. He prayed she was a secretary so he could make her his own. He didn't care what strings he had to pull; he wanted her working with him. Mrs. Hillard was looking to retire, and the thought of greeting each day with Cindy was enough to... The thought crystallized in his mind. He *was* going crazy. The cardinal rule of any office was never to become romantically involved with an employee.

He must have given her a shocked look because Cindy's gaze met his and her eyes softened with such compassion that Throne could barely breathe.

"It's all right," she whispered.

"But..."

"No," she said and pressed her fingers to his lips, silencing him.

He gave her a funny look. Could she read his thoughts as well? Was she clairvoyant? She couldn't possibly have known what he'd been thinking, yet she showed him in a glance that she understood his very soul.

"You don't need to tell me," Cindy spoke after a long moment. "I already know about Sheila."

Chapter Three

Sheila." The name seared through Thorne's mind.
Good Lord, he was practically engaged to the other
woman and here he was sitting beside Cindy and madly
plotting to keep her in his life. He thrust his face toward her, his mouth gaping open as one thought
quickly stumbled over another. He had to explain. He
had to let Cindy know—only he wasn't sure how he
was going to unscramble his own mind, let alone reassure her. It was as though Sheila meant nothing to him.
Nothing. Yet a few days before, he'd contemplated
giving her an engagement ring for Christmas. He'd
actually been entertaining the idea of marriage and
starting a family.

The twisting, churning trail of his thoughts must
have been visible in his eyes, because Cindy's gaze
softened and she smiled with such sweet understand-

ing that the panic that gripped him was instantly quelled.

He looked so astonished, so shocked, that Cindy placed her index finger across his lips. "Shh. You don't need to tell me anything; I understand."

If she did he wished to hell she'd explain things to him. Thorne felt like a scheming hypocrite. He was nearly engaged to one woman and so attracted to another he could barely take his eyes off her. Even now when she'd brought Sheila's name between them, he couldn't force himself to leave Cindy. By all that was right, he should stand up and walk away. He should escape before whatever was happening this enchanted evening could mark him. His gut reaction was that Cindy's imprint on him could well be indelible. It was crazy, the things he was thinking. Insane to want her working with him. Absurd to seriously consider dating an employee. His mother would be stunned, his father amused. They'd been after him for years to settle down, but they'd made it abundantly clear that they expected him to marry the right type of woman.

"You're angry now," Cindy said, studying the dark emotion as it wove its way across his face, pinching his eyes and mouth, drawing his brow together in a deep frown.

"Not angry," he countered. "Confused."

"Don't be."

He took her hand in his, weaving their fingers together. She had beautiful hands. Each finger was narrow and tapered, and intuitively Thorne felt the gentle comfort she would be capable of granting with a mere touch. The nails were clipped to a respectable length, neither too long nor too short. He supposed she had to keep them short in order to type properly.

"Who are you?" he asked, astonished that even her fingers could entice him.

Cindy felt the magic slowly dissipating. "I . . . I already told you."

"Cinderella?"

"Yes."

"And I'm your prince?"

"Yes." She nodded vigorously. "I've dreamed of you so often, and then I met you, and I knew you were everything my fantasies had promised."

He forced her gaze to meet his by placing his index finger beneath her chin. Studying her intense blue eyes was like looking into the crystal-clear water that ran off the mountains during spring thaw. She was incapable of deception. Unbelievably sweet. Completely innocent. She was everything he'd dared hope he'd find in a woman—yet had never believed he'd find. She was unexpected sunshine and warmth on a winter day. Laughter and excitement in the middle of a deep, dark void. Love when he least anticipated it and was least prepared to deal with it. "You claimed I disappointed you."

"That was before. Now I know who you really are, and I can hardly believe it's true."

"Oh, Cindy." He couldn't stop himself. He lowered his mouth to hers and kissed her again, wrapping his arms around her, holding her against him, savoring the feminine feel of her as she pressed her softness to his hard chest. She tasted like heaven, and her lips promised him paradise. "Cindy," he whispered against her mouth. Never had a name been more lovely. He kissed her again and drew her bottom lip gently between his teeth.

Cindy leaned into him and parted her mouth to the pressure of his tongue. She could barely breathe past the pagan beat of her heart. She feared she'd wake up any minute and discover this had all been a dream.

Thorne heaved a sigh that came all the way from the marrow of his bones and held her so close that his arms ached.

"Thorne..."

"I'm hurting you?" He relaxed the pressure instantly and ran his hands down the length of her back and up again to rest on the curve of her shoulders. His thumb stroked the pulse that was rapidly pounding near the hollow of her throat. Reluctantly he eased her away from him. "Tell me about yourself. I want to know everything."

Cindy dropped her gaze and laughed lightly to hide her uneasiness. She couldn't tell him anything. "There isn't much to tell."

She placed her hands on the side of his face and slowly rubbed his jaw. "I see such pride in you. Stubborn pride," she amended with a gentle smile. "And mind-bending determination. Were you always like this?"

Thorne could deny neither; she read him as easily as she would a billboard. He could disguise his thoughts and reactions from others, but not from Cindy. "Always, I think. My mother claims that when I was fourteen months old, I tossed my bottle against the wall and refused to drink out of anything but a cup from then on. That was only the beginning. When other children were riding tricycles, I wanted a two-wheeler. I was reading by age five and not because I was gifted. My older sisters read and I was hell-bent to do anything they could.''

"I refused to give up my blanky until I was six,'' Cindy admitted sheepishly. It had been her only comfort after her mother had died, and she'd clung to it feverishly, initially refusing to accept the love her aunt and her uncle had offered.

"You must have been a beautiful baby.''

"I had buckteeth and freckles.''

"I wore braces and corrective shoes.''

Cindy laughed. "You were always the sportsman, though, weren't you?''

Thorne's eyes momentarily clouded. "Yes.''

"Something happened.'' Cindy could see it: a flash of some memory that came so briefly that another person might have missed it.

His heart hammered relentlessly, squeezing with rare emotion. He'd hadn't thought about the accident in years. He'd only been a child. Ten years old.

Cindy saw the pain in his eyes and although she didn't understand it, she knew she had to comfort him. She lifted her hand and gently touched his face. "Tell me,'' she whispered in a low, coaxing tone. "Tell me. Tell me everything.''

Sensation raced through Thorne like wildfire. He caught her hand, raised it to his mouth and kissed her palm. "I fell from my horse. I thought I was dead, then I realized that death wouldn't hurt that much. I was barely conscious; every breath I drew was like inhaling fire.''

Cindy bit her bottom lip. The thought of Thorne in pain, even discomfort that he'd suffered years before, was more than she could bear. "Broken ribs?"

"Six, and a bruised kidney."

Her fingers tightened over his. There was more than the physical pain he was remembering; something far deeper, far more intense, punctured his memory. "What happened?"

He gave her a long, hard look. "I already told you. I fell off the horse."

"No. Afterward."

"Afterward," he repeated in a tight murmur. He remembered lying in bed in his darkened room hours later. The pain hadn't gone away. If anything, it had grown so much worse he wished he had died just so he wouldn't have to bear the agony any longer. One eye had been so severely bruised it had swollen shut. The side of his face was badly scraped, and the incredible ache in his jaw wouldn't go away. Two days later, the doctor discovered that it, too, had been broken in the fall.

His father was away much of the time, traveling for business, when Thorne was a boy, but he'd come the afternoon of the accident to see his son. Thorne had looked up at his father, grateful he was there. Tears had welled in Thorne's eyes, but instead of offering comfort, the elder Prince had spoken of what it meant to be a man and how a true man never revealed his emotions and certainly never cried.

"Thorne," Cindy prompted.

"My father forced me out of bed and into the saddle." He'd never told anyone about that incident. It made his father sound heartless and cruel. Thorndike,

Sr. was neither—only proud and stubborn like his son. Thorne paused and his eyes narrowed. "Why am I telling you this?"

"You needed to," she answered simply.

Thorne looked startled. She was right. He had needed to tell someone about the accident, only he hadn't recognized the necessity of it himself. Until tonight with Cindy. Unexpectedly, he felt like laughing.

"Let's walk," he said, coming to his feet.

Cindy joined him and he tucked her hand into the crook of his elbow, folding his hand over her fingers. "This really is an enchanted evening, isn't it?"

"Magical," she returned, her eyes smiling softly into his.

They strolled along the walkway that led around the pond. Thorne felt like singing, which of course was ridiculous. He didn't sing. Not even in the shower. "Is there some deep, dark secret about yourself you should tell me?"

"Plenty," she answered, swallowing a laugh.

"Tell me just one so I won't feel like such a fool."

"Okay." She experienced an overwhelming urge to throw back her head and laugh. "No one knows this."

"Good." Thorne was pleased to hear it.

She hesitated. "You'll probably find this amusing, but I promise you, it isn't."

"I won't laugh," he promised and crossed his heart, vowing his silence.

She regarded him steadily, uncertain she could trust him with something this silly. "I still have my blanky."

"Do you sleep with it?"

"Of course not." She was offended until she realized he was silently amused by her admission. She bit back an angry response. He'd shared something profound with her. Her threadbare blanky was a little thing. "It's tucked away in a bottom drawer."

His eyes fairly sparkled.

"Thorndike Prince, you're laughing at me!"

"I swear I'm not." He gave her a look of childlike innocence. "Tell me something more."

"Never," she vowed, a chuckle punctuating her words.

Thorne paused and draped his arm over her shoulder. He lifted his gaze to the clear night sky. Stars filled the heavens, glimmering, glinting, glistening across the tops of the skyscrapers. "It's a beautiful night."

Cindy's gaze followed his. "Shall we make a wish?"

He turned his gaze to her. "A wish?"

"Upon a star." She twisted so she stood directly in front of him. "You haven't done this in a long time, have you?"

"No." There had seldom been time for childish games. In some ways, Thorne had never been allowed to be a boy. Responsibilities had greeted him at the bassinet. He was the only son, and as he was born after two daughters, great things had been expected of him.

"Then do it now," she urged gently, tossing back her head to gaze into the heavens. She picked out the brightest star, lowered her lashes and wished with all her heart that this night would never end. "Okay," she whispered when she'd finished, "it's your turn."

He stared at her blankly. "You're sure you want me to do this?"

"Yes," she answered simply.

Like Cindy, he raised his head and studied the heavens. "You don't honestly believe in this, do you?"

"You're asking Cinderella something like that? Of course, I believe. It's required of all princesses in fairy tales."

"What should I ask for?"

It took Cindy a moment to realize that whatever Thorne wanted in life he purchased without a second thought. He probably had every material possession he could possibly want.

"Ask for something you never expected to receive," she instructed softly.

Thorne dropped his gaze to Cindy. He'd never thought to meet anyone like her. Someone so pure and good. Someone so honest and forthright. A woman who stirred his mind as well as his heart. A woman of insight and laughter. He felt like a teenager next to her, yearning to find a way to please her—to thank her for giving him this priceless gift of joy.

His eyes melted her soul. He was looking at her as she'd always imagined great heroes viewed the loves of their lives. The way Heathcliff regarded Catherine or Mr. Rochester saw Jane Eyre. The bored, cynical look that tightened his features when she'd first arrived at the party had been replaced with one of tender gentleness.

"Close your eyes," she told him when she found her voice. "You have to close your eyes to make your wish come true."

Reluctantly Thorne did as she requested, but he didn't need any stars or any wishes to be granted his lone request. Without his even asking, it had already come true: everything he'd ever wanted was standing no more than a few inches from him. And if he doubted, all he had to do was reach out and touch her. Cindy was his, and he'd found her in the nick of time. To think that only a few hours before, he'd dreaded attending this party. The thought astonished him. Now he'd thank God every day of his life that he had been there to meet Cindy.

"Have you finished?" she whispered, surprised at the inordinate amount of time he took to make his request of the heavens.

Slowly Thorne opened his eyes. "Are you going to tell me your wish?" he asked, bringing her against his side once more. He had to keep touching her to believe she was real and he wasn't in the middle of some fever-induced hallucination.

"I might as well," she said softly. "There's no possibility it will ever come true."

"Don't be so certain. I thought we'd already agreed this night is filled with magic."

"It couldn't come true." Her footsteps matched his own as they continued strolling. As much as she wished it to be, her request was an impossibility, and she'd best accept it as such. "I asked that this night would never end."

"Ah." Thorne understood her reasoning. "But in some ways it never will."

"How's that?" Cindy turned her head to better study his expression. When she'd first conceived this plan, she'd counted on the magic to work for her. Now that she saw how greatly Thorne had been affected by her schemes, she marveled at the potency of the stars to grant her wishes.

"This night will last forever," Thorne said thoughtfully.

"But how?" Cindy didn't understand because midnight loomed and she knew she must leave him. There was no turning back for Cinderella.

"It will live in our hearts."

The tear that sprang to the corner of Cindy's eye was so unexpected and so profoundly felt that she hurriedly turned her head away in an effort to hide it from Thorne. She hadn't expected ... hadn't dared to hope he would be so romantic.

"That's beautiful," she said in a choked whisper. "Prince Charming himself couldn't have said it any better."

"Only Cinderella would know that."

Cindy smiled, letting the wonder of this night dispel all doubts.

"So you're still claiming to be Cinderella?"

"Oh, yes, it's quite true."

His steps slowed. "Do you have two ugly stepsisters?"

"No," she answered, grateful he'd steered the conversation to lighter subjects.

"What about a fairy godmother?"

"A wonderful but ordinary godmother," she answered, convinced her aunt would appreciate the compliment. "But that doesn't mean she lacks magical powers."

"Did she turn the mice into horses for your carriage?"

Cindy frowned. "I don't exactly have a carriage."

"Yes, you do," Thorne said, leading her onto the sidewalk along Central Park Avenue South. Horse-drawn carriages lined the streets, seeming to wait for her command. "Your carriage awaits you, my lady," Thorne told her formally, bowing low as a knight of old would have done for his princess.

As if reading Thorne's thoughts, the middle-aged driver, who wore a black top hat, stepped forward and opened the carriage door. Cindy accepted his hand and climbed inside. The black leather cushion creaked when she sat, and Cindy tucked her dress around her. She continued to wear Thorne's overcoat and wondered guiltily if he was chilled. The warmth of the look he gave her when he climbed in after her chased away any doubt.

Sitting beside Cindy, Thorne placed his arm around her shoulders. "I've lived in Manhattan for the past six years and I've never done this."

"Me either," Cindy admitted, feeling as excited as a child.

"I may have confused the driver, however," Thorne claimed, his eyes twinkling with merriment. "I told him we wanted to survey our kingdom."

Cindy laughed. "Oh, dear, the poor man. He must think we're both crazy."

"We are, but I don't mind. Do you?" His eyes grew sober. When Cindy was with him it didn't matter if the world found his behavior amusing.

"Not in the least."

The driver jumped into the carriage box and gently urged the horse onto the street. The giant wheels at Cindy's side drowned out the sound of the horse's shoes as they clapped noisily against the pavement.

"I've always wanted to do this," Cindy admitted. "Thank you, Thorne." She laid her head upon his shoulder and drew in a deep breath. She yearned to hold on to this moment for as long as possible before having to relinquish it.

Thorne intertwined his fingers with hers and raised her hand to his mouth to brush a kiss across her knuckles. "I know so little about you."

"You know everything that's important."

"I feel like I do," he said after a moment. "I know this sounds loony, but it's as if I've known you all my life."

Cindy understood. "In some ways, I think that I might have been born for this night."

"I feel like I've been born for you."

Cindy went stock-still. It became difficult to swallow. They had only tonight. Only these few hours, and when it was midnight, she would be forced to go back to being the girl who cleaned his office. A nobody. Certainly no one who would ever interest Thorndike Prince, first vice president. Her mind spun with countless possibilities, but they all ended with the same shattering reality. She couldn't change who she was, and he couldn't alter the man he had become. There could be no middle ground for them.

"You're terribly quiet all of a sudden," Thorne observed. He liked having her close to him. He loved touching her and kissing her. But the fascination he felt for her wasn't physical. The only word he could think of that might describe his feelings was *spiritual*. Something buried deep within him had reached out and met a significant inner part of the woman at his side. His inner personality had connected with hers. With her, he experienced a wholeness, a rightness that had been missing from his life.

"Let's not think beyond anything but this night," Cindy said softly. Her mind was conjuring up ways in which she could meet him again, but she quickly realized the impossibility of it all. As it was, she had stolen this one night. There could be no others. Ever. A sadness surrounded her heart, pressing against her with such heaviness that she nearly gave up breathing, the effort was so great.

"We'll share forever," Thorne returned quickly. "And all the nights for the rest of our lives." He knew he was rushing her. Good God, they'd only met a few hours before, and he was practically asking her what names she planned to give their children. The thought stunned him. He, Thorndike Prince, who had always been described as an unemotional, hard-hearted cynic, was talking like a lovesick teenager. And loving it. He'd been ignorant before meeting Cindy. Stupid. Now that he'd met her, he understood what drove men to impossible feats in the name of love. He'd walk over hot coals to get to Cindy. Hell, he'd walk across water just to be at her side. Nothing would stop him now that he'd discovered her.

"I want you to meet my family." He shocked himself by making the suggestion.

"Your family?" Cindy repeated, stunned.

"Yes." He'd talk to both his mother and his father first. They'd be surprised, of course, since they'd been expecting him to announce he was marrying Sheila. Sheila. He nearly laughed aloud. He couldn't even remember what the other woman looked like.

His parents could be his and Cindy's biggest hurdle. But once they met her they wouldn't question his actions. After the initial shock his mother would love her,

Thorne was certain of that. His father was another matter, but given time, he would respect Thorne's decision. Things could get a bit sticky with Sheila, but she was a reasonable woman. She wanted what was best for Thorne, and as soon as he explained, Thorne was convinced the other woman would understand.

Within a matter of hours a secretary with a saucy grin had turned his life upside down. And Thorne loved it.

"I . . . can't meet your family." Cindy's mind was in turmoil.

"Of course you can. They're going to love you."

"Thorne—"

"Stop." He pressed his finger across her lips just as she'd done to him earlier. "Here," he said, and placed her hand over his heart. "Feel how excited and happy I am. I feel alive for the first time in years. You've done that for me. I want to laugh and sing and dance, and I never do any of those things."

"But, I can't—"

"I know I'm probably going a thousand times too fast for you. I realize it all sounds crazy, but I've been waiting years for you. Years." He framed her face with his hands as his gaze studied hers. His thumbs ran over his lips before he kissed her with infinite gentleness. His mouth lingered over hers as if he couldn't get his fill of her and never would. "What took you so long, Cindy, love? What took you so very long?"

Cindy swallowed a sob at the tenderness she saw in his eyes. "Thorne, please . . . don't . . ."

His mouth stopped her, kissing her again until her senses spun at breakneck speed, careening down a slope of reality. There was no question of refusing herself the luxury of his touch. Nor was there a question of disillusioning him. Soon enough he would discover the truth. Soon enough he would know she wasn't who she pretended to be. She was no princess. No royal blue blood flowed through her veins. Her family name wasn't going to cause any banker's heart to react with excitement.

"I'd be honored to meet your family," she said softly.

"Tomorrow, then."

"Whenever you wish." She couldn't meet his eye, knowing there were no tomorrows for them.

They had so little time together. So little time. She couldn't ruin everything now. Maybe it was wrong not to tell him she was the janitorial worker who cleaned his office and that she had no intention of embarrassing him in front of his family. But it couldn't be any more wrong than crashing the party and seeking out Thorndike Prince in the first place.

The carriage driver paused to clear his throat. Irritated, Thorne broke away from Cindy and noted they'd completed the circle and were back.

"Shall we go around again?" On the first trip, he had gotten her to agree to meet his family. He'd seen the reluctance in her eyes and realized how much the thought had intimidated her. Yet she'd agreed. He yearned to hold her and assure her he would never leave her, that with a little time and patience his family would be as impressed with her as he was.

Somewhere in the distance a clock began to chime. Cindy paused, counting the night-piercing tones that seemed to peal on endlessly. "Midnight," she cried, her heart beating frantically. "It's midnight. I've...I've got to leave. I'm sorry...so sorry."

"Cindy." Thorne reached out for her, but already she was rushing away. He ran a few steps, his pace matching hers. "I'll take you home. Don't worry about missing your ride—I'll see you safely home."

Tears filled her eyes as she handed him his coat and paused to wrap her arms around him, hugging him with all the emotion stored in her heart. "You don't understand."

She was right about that, Thorne mused. She looked stricken—frightened and so unbelievably unhappy that he longed to ease whatever pain she was suffering.

"It was the most wonderful night of my life. I'll...remember it, and I'll always...always remember you."

"You won't get a chance to forget me." He tried to keep her with him, but she whirled around and picked up her skirts, racing away as though the very demons of hell were in wild pursuit.

Stunned into immobility, Thorne watched her race into traffic. She'd crossed the busy street and was halfway down the sidewalk, when she turned around abruptly. "Thank you," she yelled, raising her hand to wave. "Thank you for making all my dreams come true." She covered her mouth with her hand and even from the distance Thorne could see she was weeping. She ran then in earnest, sprinting to the corner. The instant she reached it a long black limousine pulled up. As if by magic, the door opened and Cindy slid inside. The limo was gone before Thorne had a chance to react.

"Sir."

For a moment Thorne didn't respond to the voice beckoning him.

"She dropped these." The carriage driver handed Thorne two pearl combs.

The older man with the black top hat stared at Thorne. "Had to be home by midnight, did she?"

"Yes," Thorne responded without looking at the other man.

"Sounds like Cinderella."

"That's who she said she was."

The other man chuckled. "Then you must be Prince Charming."

Still, Thorne didn't move. "I am."

The carriage driver found that all the more amusing. "Sure, fella. And I'm Mr. Rockefeller himself."

Chapter Four

The first thing Thorne thought about when he woke early the following morning was Cindy. He'd drifted into a deep, restful sleep, picturing her sweet face, and he woke cursing himself for not getting her phone number. Being forced into waiting an entire day to see her again was nearly intolerable, but she'd left in such a maddening rush that he hadn't thought to ask her for it. Now he was paying the price for his own lack of forethought.

After he'd showered, he stood in a thick robe in front of his fourteenth-floor window. Manhattan stretched out before him like a concrete jungle, bold and brash. The crazy thing was how much he felt like singing. He'd been shocked to find himself humming in the shower. He gripped with both hands the towel that was draped around his neck and expelled a long, thoughtful sigh. It was almost as if he'd been reborn. The world below buzzed with activity. Cars crowded the streets. A Circle Line tourist boat cruised around the island. Funny, he hadn't paid much attention to the Hudson River or seaport or any of the other sights in a long while. Now they sparkled like a thousand facets in a flawless diamond. It was ridiculous to believe he might be in love, but he felt breathless with excitement just thinking about Cindy.

The phone rang and Thorne reached for it expectantly. It was unrealistic to hope it was Cindy calling, and yet he nearly sighed with disappointment when his mother's voice greeted him.

"Thorne, it's your mother."

"Good morning, Mother."

"You certainly sound in a cheerful mood. How was the Christmas Ball?"

"Fabulous."

"Did Sheila attend with you?"

"No, she couldn't get away." His mother liked to keep close tabs on her children. Thorne tolerated her frequent calls because she was his mother, and her motivation was innocent enough, although he'd made it clear that his personal life was his own. She wanted him settled, sedately married and producing enough grandchildren to keep her occupied. His sisters had done their share and now it was his turn.

He spoke again, remembering that he'd asked Cindy to meet his family. "Mother, listen, I'm pleased you phoned. There's someone I'd like to bring to the house. Would it be possible to have her to dinner soon?"

"Her?"

"Yes, if it's not inconvenient, perhaps we could set it up for Christmas week."

"Do you have some exciting news for us, darling?"

Thorne weighed his words. "I suppose you could say so." He'd met the woman he planned to share his life with. It didn't get much more exciting than that, but he wasn't about to announce that to his family. After all, he'd just met Cindy. They'd scoff at him, and even Thorne had to admit he was behaving like a romantic fool.

"I believe your father and I may have already guessed your news." His mother's voice was soft and lilting with excitement.

"It's not what you think, Mother." Thorne paused and chuckled. "Or *who* you think, for that matter. I met someone wonderful last night...someone very special. I suppose it was a bit presumptuous of me, but I invited her over to meet you and Dad." The invitation alone must have been a shock to his mother, Thorne realized. He rarely introduced his lady friends to his family.

The short silence that followed was heavy. "This someone you met...she isn't by chance...Sheila?"

"Her name is Cindy, and we met at the Christmas Ball." Even his own mother would assume he'd lost his mind if he were to tell her that the minute he'd held Cindy, he'd known she was going to be special in his life.

"Cindy." His mother repeated it slowly, as though testing it on her tongue. "What's her last name?"

Thorne realized his mother was really inquiring about her family. He hated to admit it, but his own mother was a terrible snob.

"Surely she has a surname?" his mother taunted, obviously displeased about this unexpected turn of events.

Thorne hesitated. Now that he stopped and thought about it, he realized he didn't know Cindy's surname. "I don't believe she told me."

"You don't know her last name?"

"I just told you that, Mother. But it isn't any problem. I'll see her again Monday morning." Even as he said it, it sounded like an eternity, and Thorne wasn't entirely convinced he could wait. "She's an employee of Oakes-Jenning."

Another lengthy pause followed. "You haven't said anything to Sheila?"

"Of course not, I only met Cindy last night. Listen, Mother, I probably am making a mistake even mentioning her to you like this, but—"

"It's just a shock, that's all," his mother responded calmly, having regained her composure. "Do me a favor, son, and don't say anything to Sheila yet."

"But, Mother—"

"I wouldn't want you to mislead the poor girl, but you might save yourself a considerable amount of heartache until you and... What was her name again?"

"Cindy."

"Ah, yes, Cindy. It would be better if you sorted out your feelings regarding Cindy before you say something to Sheila that you'll regret later."

"Cindy knows all about Sheila."

"Yes, but Sheila doesn't know about Cindy, and my guess is that it would be best to let this new... relationship simmer for a time until you're sure of your feelings."

Thorne's jaw tightened. He'd been foolish to mention Cindy to his mother. It was too soon. Later, when they saw how much he'd changed, they'd want to know the reason; he could explain Cindy then.

"Thorne?" His mother prompted. "Do you agree?"

For a moment he had to stop and think what she was asking him to agree to. "I won't say anything to Sheila," he promised.

"Good." Her relief came in the form of an exaggerated sigh.

"You must have phoned for some reason, Mother."

"Oh, yes," she said and laughed nervously. "It was about Christmas Day...I was wondering if you minded...if I invited Sheila."

"Perhaps it would be best if you didn't." Although Christmas was only a little more than a week away, Thorne had hoped to share this special day with Cindy. Christmas and every day in between.

The pause that followed told Thorne his objection came too late.

"I'm afraid...I happened to run into her yesterday when I was shopping...and, oh, dear, this is going to be a bit messy."

"Sheila's already been invited," Thorne finished for his mother. He closed his eyes to the cloudburst of anger that rained over him and quickly forgave her interfering ways. She hadn't meant to cause a problem. It must have seemed only natural to extend the invitation when he'd recently indicated he was considering marrying the other woman.

"Will that be so very uncomfortable, darling?"

"Don't worry about it, Mother. I'm sure everything will work out fine." Cindy would understand, Thorne realized. She was an incredible person who revealed no tendencies toward unreasonable jealousy.

"I do apologize, but your father and I both thought Sheila would be joining our family...permanently."

"I know, Mother, this change of heart is rather unexpected."

The remainder of the conversation with his mother was brief and Thorne hung up the phone, more confident than ever about his powerful feelings for Cindy. Just remembering the way she'd strolled up to him at the ball and announced that she was Cinderella brought a quivering smile to the corners of his mouth. And then she'd told him what a sorry disappointment he was to her. Thorne laughed out loud. Monday morning couldn't come soon enough to suit him. Not nearly soon enough.

Cindy woke to a pounding headache. Her head throbbed with pain and she placed her hand over her eyes to block out the light. She didn't suffer from these often, but when she did they were debilitating. Her mouth felt dry and her tongue swollen. Carefully she rolled onto her back and stared at the ceiling, waiting for the discomfort to pass.

The evening with Thorne had been so much more than she'd dared to dream. She hadn't been able to sleep for hours after her Uncle Sal had dropped her off in Little Italy. She lay in bed and continued to relive every part of the evening. The night had been perfect—from their awkward beginning when she'd introduced herself, to the tenderness she'd seen in his gaze when he looked down on her in the carriage. An aching sob built up in her chest until she was forced to bite down on her bottom lip to hold it inside.

She'd been wrong to play the role of Cinderella. It would have been so much easier never to have met Thorne. Now she was forever doomed to hold this ache within her breast for having so flippantly tempted fate.

When she'd arrived home, even before she'd undressed, Cindy had sat on the end of her bed and tried to picture Thorne in her home. The mental image was so discordant that she'd been forced to cast the thought from her mind. If Thorne were to see this apartment and the earthy family she loved, he would be embarrassed. Thorne Prince didn't know what it meant to live from paycheck to paycheck or to "make do" when money was tight. He might as well live on another planet in a neighboring solar system, he was so far removed from her way of life.

"Cindy." Her aunt knocked gently at the bedroom door. "Are you awake?"

Cindy sat up awkwardly and leaned against her headboard. "I'm up... come on in."

Slowly, her aunt opened the door. Her eyes met Cindy's. "It's nearly noon. Are you feeling ill?"

It was unusual for Cindy to stay in bed for any reason. "A headache."

Aunt Theresa sat on the edge of the bed and brushed the hair away from Cindy's brow. "Did you have a good time last night?" she asked softly, studying her niece.

Cindy's gaze dropped to the patchwork quilt that served as her bedspread. "I had a wonderful time."

"Did Cinderella meet her prince?"

Cindy's eyes glistened at the memory. "I spent most of the evening with him."

"And was he everything she expected?"

Cindy nodded because speaking was impossible. She leaned forward enough to rest her head on her aunt's shoulder.

"And now?" The older woman probed.

"And now Cinderella realizes what a terrible fool she was because at midnight she turned back into plain, simple Cindy Territo." A tear scorched her cheek and her arms circled her aunt's neck. As she had as a child, Cindy needed the warmth and security of her aunt's love.

"My darling girl, you are neither plain nor simple."

Cindy sniffled and sadly shook her head. "Compared to other women he knows, I am."

"But he liked you."

"He thought I was a secretary."

"Nevertheless he must have been impressed to have spent the evening in your company. Does it matter so much if you're a secretary or a charwoman?"

"Unfortunately, it does."

"It seems to me you're selling your prince short," her aunt said soothingly, stroking the back of Cindy's head. "If he's everything you've said, it wouldn't matter in the least."

Cindy said nothing. She couldn't answer her aunt's questions. Her own doubts were overwhelming.

"Do you plan to see him again?" Theresa asked, after a thoughtful moment.

Cindy closed her eyes to the searing disappointment and emotional pain. "Never," she whispered.

Monday morning Thorne walked crisply into his office fifteen minutes ahead of his usual routine. Mrs. Hillard, his secretary, looked up from the work on her desk, revealing mild surprise that her employer was early.

"Good morning, Mrs. Hillard. It's a beautiful day, isn't it?"

His secretary's mouth dropped open. "It's barely above freezing and the weathermen are forecasting a snowstorm by midafternoon."

"I love snow," Thorne continued, undaunted.

Mrs. Hillard rolled out her chair and stood. "Are you feeling all right, sir?"

"I'm feeling absolutely wonderful."

"Can I get you some coffee?"

"Please." Thorne strolled toward his desk. "And contact Wells in personnel, would you?"

"Right away." A minute later she delivered his coffee. The red light on his phone was lit, and Thorne sat in his chair and reached for the receiver.

"This is Thorndike Prince," he began in clipped tones. "Would you kindly check your files for the name Cindy. She works on the executive floor. I'd like her full name and the office number."

"Cindy?" The tinny voice of the personnel director came back over the phone.

"Unfortunately, I don't have her surname."

"This may take some time, Mr. Prince; I'll have to phone you back."

Thorne thumped his fingers against the top of his desk in an effort to disguise his impatience. "No problem. I'll wait to hear from you." He replaced the receiver and leaned back in his chair, holding the coffee in both hands. He gazed out the window and noted for the first time the thick, angry clouds that threatened the sky. A snowstorm, Mrs. Hillard had said. Terrific! He'd take Cindy for a walk in the falling snow and warm her with kisses. They'd go back to the park and feed the pigeons and then to his apartment and drink mulled wine. He'd spent one restless day without her and he wasn't about to waste another. His head was bursting with things he wanted to tell her, things he found vitally important to share. Today he'd learn everything he could about her. Once he knew everything, he'd take her in his arms and tell her the magic hadn't quit working. The spell she'd cast on him hadn't faded and couldn't. If anything, it had grown stronger with every passing minute.

The phone pealed and he jerked the receiver off its cradle. "Prince here."

"This is Mr. Wells from personnel."

"Yes."

"Sir—" he paused and cleared his throat "—I've checked all our records and I don't find anyone with the name Cindy or Cynthia employed on the executive floor."

"Then look again," Thorne said stiffly. The incompetence he was forced to deal with on a day-to-day basis was enough to try the patience of any man.

"Sir, I've checked the files three times."

"Then I suggest you do so again." Thorne slammed down the phone. The only way he was going to get Cindy's name was to go down there himself and locate it. Nothing irritated him more than this kind of flaming stupidity.

A half hour later, Thorne was forced to agree with Wells. There wasn't a secretary in the entire company with the name Cindy. Thorne slammed the filing-cabinet drawer shut with unnecessary force.

"Who was in charge of the Christmas Ball?" he demanded.

Mr. Wells, a diminutive man who wore a bow tie and glasses, cleared his throat. "I was, Mr. Prince."

"The ball was by invitation only; is that correct?"

"Yes, sir, I received my instructions from—"

"I want the list."

"The list?" He pulled out a file and handed Thorne several sheets of paper. "The name of every employee who received an invitation is here, except one and—"

"Who?" Angrily Thorne whirled around to face the other man, prepared to do whatever was necessary to learn the name.

"Myself," Wells admitted in a choked, startled voice.

Thorne's gaze scanned the list, then again much more slowly, carefully examining each name. No one named Cindy was there.

"How many extra invitations were printed?"

"A dozen... I have a list here." Wells pulled a sheet of paper from the file and Thorne took it and counted the names typed on it. Exactly twelve.

"Sir... perhaps this Cindy crashed the party.... There are ways," he stammered. "The hotel staff does all it can to assure that only those with an invitation are granted admission, but... it's been known to happen."

"Crashed the ball..." Thorne repeated, stunned. He paused and rubbed a hand over his face. That was exactly what had happened. The instant he heard Wells say it, he recognized the truth. "Thank you for your trouble."

"It was no problem, Mr. Prince. Perhaps if you could describe the girl, I could go through our files and locate several pictures. It could be that she is employed by Oakes-Jenning, but is assuming another name."

Thorne barely heard the other man. "That won't be necessary." He turned and left the office, reaching his own without remembering having stepped into the elevator.

Mrs. Hillard stood when he entered the room, her hands filled with the mail. Thorne gave her a look that told her he'd deal with his correspondence later, and she sat back down again.

For two days he'd been living in a dreamworld, Thorne realized. He'd been acting the part of an idiotic, romantic fool. The joyful expectation drained out of him and was replaced with a grim determination not to allow such folly to overtake him a second time. He'd put Cindy out of his mind and his heart as easily as he'd instilled her there. She was a fraud who had taken delight in duping him. Well, her plans had worked beyond her greatest expectation. He slumped into his chair and turned to look at the sky. Mrs. Hillard was right. The weather was terrible, but then so was the day.

Chapter Five

Thorne's violent sneeze tore the tissue in half. He reached for another in the nick of time. His eyes were running, he was so congested he could barely breathe and he had a fever. He felt thoroughly miserable, and it wasn't all due to this wretched cold. He'd gotten it the night he'd given Cindy his coat. Cindy. She haunted his dreams and filled his every waking thought. He wanted to hate her, shout at her and . . . and take her in his arms and hold her to him for all time. There were moments when he despised her, and then there were other times, usually at night, when he'd lie back and close his eyes. She came to him then, in those quiet moments, and tortured him, playing back every minute of their enchanted evening together. He'd be on the ballroom floor with her in his arms; a second later he'd recall with vivid clarity the agony in her eyes as she tearfully told him goodbye. When she repeated over and over how sorry she was, the words seemed to echo around the canyons of his mind like piercing rifle shots in the night.

Thorne picked up the pearl comb and fingered it for the thousandth time in the past five days. He'd kept it with him constantly, seeking some clue from it, some solace. He found neither. He'd taken it to a jeweler and learned it was a moderately inexpensive comb that was perhaps twenty-five years old—certainly of little value beyond sentimental. It wasn't as if he could take it around the executive floor and try it on women's heads to see if it would fit. Cinderella had left him a useless white elephant. He couldn't trace her with a common pearl hair clip.

Other than the comb, Thorne had nothing with which to find Cindy. The crazy part was that he wasn't completely convinced he wanted to see her again. She'd lied to him, played him for a fool and mercilessly shattered his dreams—serious crimes for a woman he'd known for less than ten hours...and yet he couldn't stop thinking about her. Every minute. Every day. God knew, he wanted to cast her from his mind—to condemn her to the deepest, darkest reaches of hell . Then and only then could she fully appreciate what she'd done to him.

Thorne's thoughts were followed by another thunderous sneeze. He pressed the intercom button and summoned his secretary. "Did you get that orange juice?" he demanded.

"It's on its way," she informed him in a crisp, businesslike tone.

"Good." Thorne pulled open the top desk drawer and reached for the aspirin bottle. Lord, he was miserable, in both body and spirit.

Cindy inhaled a deep breath and forced herself into Thorne's office. It was torture to be inside the room where he spent so much of his time. She could feel his presence so strongly that she kept looking over her shoulder, convinced he was there, standing behind her. She wondered what he would say to her—if he hated her or if he even thought about her—then decided she'd rather not know. Her heart felt weighed down with a multitude of regrets.

Pushing Thorne out of her thoughts, she ran the feather duster over the top of his desk. Something small and white fell from the desktop and rolled onto the carpet. Cindy bent over and picked it up. A pearl. She held it in the palm of her hand and stared at it with open fascination. Thorne had her mother's combs! Cindy had thought they were lost to her forever. Not until she was home did she realize they'd fallen from her hair, and she'd been devastated over their loss. She had so few of her mother's personal possessions that losing even one was monumental.

"What's that?" Vanessa asked, standing in the open doorway, her feather duster stored in her hip pocket.

Cindy's hand closed over the pearl. Knowing that Thorne had the combs gave her a secure feeling. "A pearl," she said, tucking it inside the pocket of her coveralls.

Vanessa studied her closely. "Do you think it might be from your mother's combs?"

"I'm sure it is." If she were to leave part of herself with him, then something that was of such high value to her was fitting.

"Then your prince must have them."

Cindy nodded, comforted immeasurably by the information. "One, at least."

"How do you plan to get it back?"

"I don't," Cindy said and continued dusting, praying Vanessa would return to her own tasks so Cindy could keep her thoughts to herself.

"You aren't going to get them from him? That's crazy. You were sick about losing those combs."

"I know."

"Well, good grief, Cindy girl, here's the perfect opportunity for you to see your handsome prince a second time. Grab it, for heaven's sake!"

Cindy's mouth quivered. "I don't want to see him again."

"You might be able to fool your family, but you won't have such an easy time with me," Vanessa pressed, her mouth grim and her eyes revealing her disapproval. "You told me the ball was the happiest, most exciting night of your life."

Cindy's back stiffened. The warm, fairy-tale sensations the ball had aroused were supposed to last a lifetime, and instead the evening had left Cindy yearning for many, many more. "The night was everything I dreamed, but don't you see? I was playing a role... I was glamorous and sophisticated and someone totally different from the Cindy Territo you see now. The show closed, the part is cancelled and I've gone back to being just plain me: Cindy Territo, janitorial worker, part-time student."

"Cindy—the woman in love."

"Stop it, Vanessa!" she cried and whirled around to face her friend. "Adults don't fall in love after one night. Not true love—it just doesn't happen!"

Suavely Vanessa crossed her arms and leaned her hip against the side of Thorne's rosewood desk. "That's not what I hear."

Cindy snorted softly. "That's not love...that's hormones. It wasn't like that with Thorne and me; I don't think I can explain it...I've never felt anything like this with any man." She couldn't find the words to explain to her friend that what she shared with Thorne wasn't physical, but spiritual.

"And you're convinced it can't be love?" Vanessa taunted.

"It's impossible... I don't want to talk about him or that night again. I...we have to put it out of our minds." She reached for Thorne's wastepaper basket and unceremoniously dumped it inside her cart. When she saw the contents her eyes widened with self-recriminations. "Vanessa, look." She picked up a discarded aspirin box and another for a multisymptom-cold remedy. "Thorne's sick."

"He must have gone through a whole box of tissues from the looks of it."

"Oh, no." Cindy sagged into his chair, lovingly stroking the arm as though it were his fevered brow. She longed to be with him. "The night of the ball," she began, her voice strained with regret, "when we went into the park, he gave me his coat so I wouldn't catch cold."

"At a price, it seems."

Cindy's face went pale, and she looked distractedly at her friend before turning her head away and closing her eyes. "It's all my fault. Christmas is only a few days away.... Oh, dear, I did this to him."

"What do you plan to do about it?"

"What can I do?" If Cindy was miserable before, it was nothing compared to the guilt she suffered now, knowing her prince was ill because of something she'd done.

"Make him some chicken soup and take it to him," Vanessa suggested thoughtfully.

Cindy's eyes widened. "I couldn't."

"This is the same woman who sauntered up to Thorndike Prince and announced he was a sad disappointment to her?"

"One and the same," Cindy returned miserably.

Vanessa shook her head and frowned. "You could have fooled me."

If anybody was a fool, Cindy determined the following afternoon, it was she. She'd spent the morning chopping vegetables into precisely even pieces and adding them to a steaming pot of stewing chicken while her aunt made up a batch of thick, homemade noodles.

"Maybe I should have Tony deliver it to him for me," Cindy suggested, eyeing her aunt speculatively.

"Tony and Maria are going to a movie, and you can bet that your prince isn't going to hand over those combs to my son without getting whatever information he could out of him." The way she was regarding Cindy suggested that Thorne would use fair means or foul to find out what he could.

"Thorne wouldn't hurt anyone," Cindy defended him righteously, and from the quick smile that lit up the older woman's features, Cindy realized she'd fallen neatly into her aunt's trap.

"Then you shouldn't have any qualms about visiting him. It's not Tony or anyone else he wants to see— it's you."

Cindy raised questioning eyes to the woman who had so lovingly raised her. "I'm not entirely convinced he does want to see me."

"He kept the combs, didn't he?"

"Yes, but that doesn't mean anything."

"No man is going to carry around a pair of women's hair combs without a reason."

"Oh, Aunt Theresa, I feel like such an idiot. What if he hates me? What if—"

"Will you stop with the what ifs! The soup is finished. Take it to him and go from there."

"But…" She strove to keep the telltale emotion from her voice. But it wouldn't take a fortune-teller to see that she was as nervous as a cat in a roomful of rocking chairs. Today…if she saw Thorne, there would be no fancy gown with dimmed lights to create an illusion of beauty and worldliness. No moonlight and magic to entice him. Her plaid wool skirt, shell-knit sweater and leather pumps would tell him everything.

Theresa caught her by the shoulders. "Stop being so nervous, it's not like you!"

Cindy forced a smile and nodded. She'd go to him because she must. Her actions were already mapped out in her mind. She'd arrive at his apartment, give him the soup and tell him how sorry she was that he'd gotten a cold. Then, depending on how he responded to her, she'd ask for her mother's combs. But only if he showed signs of being pleased to see her. Somehow she doubted he would.

The television droned in the background, but Thorne couldn't force any interest in the silly game shows that ran one after another. They, however, were only slightly less boring than the soap operas that aired on the other channels. He felt hot, then chilled. Sick and uncomfortable. Sleepy from medication and wide-awake. It was only three days until Christmas and he had all the love and goodwill of an ill-tempered, cantankerous grinch!

The small tree that decorated the corner of the living room was testimony to his own folly. He'd enthusiastically put it up the day after meeting Cindy, and now it sat there taunting him, reminding him what a fool he was to believe in romantic dreams. In three days' time he would be obligated to arrive at his parents' home and face them and Sheila. The thought was not pleasant. All he wanted to do was bury his head in the sand and insist the world leave him alone!

He sighed and reached for a glass of grapefruit juice and another cold tablet. Discarded cold remedies crowded the surface of his glass coffee table. He'd taken one pillow from his bed and stripped away the bedspread in an effort to get comfortable in the living room.

The doorbell chimed and he twisted around and glared at it with open hostility.

Seemingly undaunted, the bell rang a second time. "Go away," he shouted. The last thing he wanted was company.

This time the ring was followed by loud knocking.

Furious, he shoved the covers aside and stormed to the front door. With equal force he jerked it open and glared angrily at the young woman who stood before him. "I said go away!" he shouted, in no mood to be civil. "I don't want to..." His voice faded to a mere croak. "Cindy?" He was too shocked, too stunned to do anything, even breathe. The first thing that came to his mind was to haul her into his arms and not let her leave until she told him who she was. But the impulse was followed immediately by an all-consuming anger. His face went hard as he glared at her with contempt.

Cindy stood frozen in front of him, unable to force a coherent word from her vocal cords. A rush of color heated her face. This was a hundred times worse than she'd imagined. Thorne hated her. Dismayed and disheartened, she handed him the large paper sack. "I...learned you were sick."

"What's this?" Knowing her, he could well suspect arsenic.

"Chicken soup."

Thorne's eyes lit up with sardonic amusement. She resembled a frightened rabbit standing in front of a hungry wolf. He wanted her to fret and wondered how anyone could look so innocent and so completely guileless when he knew her to be a liar and a cheat. "You might as well come in," he said gruffly, stepping aside to allow her entrance.

"I can only stay a minute," she said shakily.

"I wouldn't dream of inviting you to stay longer," he answered, in an effort to be cruel. He was rewarded when he watched the color drain from her soft features. Good. He wanted to hurt her. He wanted her to experience just a taste of the hell she'd put him through.

She caught her breath and nodded, saying without words that she understood.

He set the soup on the coffee table and slumped onto the white leather sofa. "I won't apologize for the mess, but as you evidently heard, I haven't been feeling well." He motioned toward the matching chair across from him. "I know what you want."

Surprise rounded her deep blue eyes. "You do?"

"It's the combs, isn't it?"

Cindy nodded and sat on the edge of the cushion, folding her hands primly in her lap. She clasped her fingers together so tightly that she was certain she'd cut off her circulation. "They were my mother's . . . You have them?"

"Both."

She sighed with relief. "I thought I'd lost them."

"You knew damn good and well I had them."

Cindy opened her mouth to argue with him but quickly closed it. He couldn't believe anything but ill of her, and she couldn't blame him.

"What? No heated defense?"

"None. You have the right to hate me. I lied to you, but not in the way you think."

"You're sure as hell no secretary."

"No, but if you remember, I never said I was."

"But you didn't stop me from thinking that."

Cindy dropped her eyes to her clenched hands. "As I said before, you have every right to be angry, but if it's any consolation to you—I am deeply and truly sorry."

His gaze narrowed, condemning her. "Such innocent eyes. Who would have guessed that such deception, such cleverness lay just below the surface? You,
my dear, should be employed by the War Department.
Your country would be well served by your deceitful-
ness."

Cindy clamped her teeth together with such force
that her jaw ached. Every word was a slap in her face
and it hurt, it hurt so terribly. His eyes were so cold and
filled with such contempt. "If I could have the
combs... I'll be on my way."

"Not quite yet." He stood and joined her, pulling
her to her feet. "You owe me something for all the lies
you told... for deceiving me into thinking you were
kind and good." For filling his head with dreams and
shattering the unspoken promises she'd given him so
freely.

Frightened, Cindy drew back sharply.

His eyes narrowed fiercely on her flushed face and
his hands tightened around her upper arm. He pulled
her against him and slanted his mouth over hers, mercilessly moving his lips against hers.

Cindy went still with shock, giving up the struggle,
letting him do as he would. Fighting would only ag-
gravate him.

Thorne felt her submission and the distress that
coursed through her veins as her heart pounded against
his own. He loosened his grip and drew back slowly.
She'd gone deathly pale, and he was instantly filled
with overwhelming regret. He dropped his hands and
watched as she took a stumbling step away from him.

"I apologize for that," he said hoarsely, condemning himself. He was wrong about her. She wasn't cold

and calculating, but warm and generous. It was all there for him to read in her clear, blue eyes. Her chin shook slightly and those magical eyes stared up at him, glimmering with deep hurt. He longed to soothe away the hurt he had inflicted. Utterly defeated, he turned and walked away. "I'll get the combs."

Thorne hesitated halfway down the hall that led to his bedroom. The floor seemed to pitch and heave under him, and he sagged against the wall in an effort to keep from falling. He knew it was the medication—the doctor had warned him about the dizzying effect.

"Thorne..." Cindy was at his side, wrapping an arm around his waist, trying to support him.

"I'll be fine in a minute."

Her hold tightened. "You're sick."

His breathless chuckle revealed his amusement. "Are you always so perceptive?"

"No." She tried to help him. "Let me get you into bed."

"Those are misleading words, Cinderella. I'm sure your fairy godmother would be shocked."

"Quit joking, I'm serious."

He turned his head and his gaze pinned hers. "So am I."

"You're to sick to make love."

"Wanna bet?"

"Thorne!" Her face filled with hot color. As best she could, Cindy directed him into the bedroom. The huge king-size bed dominated the middle of the room and was a mess of tangled sheets and blankets. She left him long enough to pull back the covers and fluff up the pillow.

Because he felt so incredibly weak, Thorne sat on the edge of the mattress and ran a weary hand over his face. Under normal circumstances he would have been humiliated to have a woman fuss over him like this, but nothing about his relationship with Cindy was the least bit conventional.

"Here, let me help you," she insisted, urging him to lie down.

"No." He brushed her hand away.

"You need to rest."

"No," he repeated, louder this time.

"Thorne, please, you're running a fever."

"If I do fall asleep," he said, holding her gaze, "you'll be gone when I wake." His mouth curved into a sad smile. "Will you promise to stay?"

Cindy hesitated.

"It's your fault I'm sick." A little guilt went a long way when used properly.

"I'll stay until you wake."

"Do you promise?"

She nodded.

"Say it, Cindy."

"I'll be here," she cried, angry that he couldn't trust her. "I wouldn't dream of leaving you like this."

He fell against the pillow and released a long sigh. "Good," he said and closed his eyes. For the first time in days he felt right. From the moment Cindy had left him standing in the park, it was as though a part of himself had been missing. Now she was here, so close that all he had to do was reach out and touch her to be whole again.

Standing at his side, Cindy drew the covers over his shoulders and lingered beside the bed. She wouldn't leave the room until she was sure he was asleep. He looked almost childlike, lying on his side, his brow relaxed and smooth. The harsh lines around his mouth were gone, as were the ones that fanned out about his eyes.

A minute later, his lashes flittered open and he looked around, startled.

"I'm here," she whispered and ran her hand across his brow to reassure him.

"Lie down with me," he pleaded and shifted to the far side of the bed, leaving more than ample room for her slim body.

"Thorne, I can't."

"Please." His voice was barely discernible, hardly more than a whisper.

No one word could ever be more seductive. "I shouldn't."

He answered her by gently patting the mattress at his side; his eyes were still closed. "I need you," he said softly.

"Oh, Thorne." She pressed her lips tightly together and slowly slipped off her shoes. He was blackmailing her and she didn't like it one bit. As soon as he was well she'd let him know in no uncertain terms what she thought of his underhanded methods.

Keeping as close to edge of the bed as possible without falling off, Cindy eased herself onto the mattress, lying stiff and tense at his side. Thorne was under the covers while she remained on top, but that did little to diminish her misgivings.

Gradually, so that she was hardly aware of what he was doing, Thorne eased himself closer to her so he could feel the warmth of her body against his. Sleep was so wonderfully inviting. He slipped his arm over her ribs and brought her close, cuddling her. He felt the tension leave her limbs, and for the first time since the Monday following the Christmas Ball, Thorne Prince smiled.

Cindy woke two hours later, stunned that she'd slept. The room was dark and she lay watching the shadows dance on the bedroom walls, thinking. Her mind was crowded with conflicting thoughts. She should leave him while she could, with her heart intact; but she'd promised him she wouldn't. No matter what the consequences, she wouldn't lie to him again. She couldn't live with herself if she did.

As gently as possible, Cindy slipped from his arms and tiptoed across the plush carpet. Clothes littered the floor and she automatically picked them up as she made her way out of the room. She found towels in the bathroom and added those to the load of shirts in the washing machine.

Dirty dishes filled the kitchen sink, and, humming as she worked, Cindy placed those in the dishwasher and turned it on as well. The pots and pans, she scrubbed by hand. She had finished those when she turned around and discovered Thorne, standing in the middle of the kitchen, watching her.

"I'd thought you'd left," he murmured, and rubbed a hand over his eyes. He'd woken to find her gone and momentary terror had gripped his heart. It wasn't until he'd realized she was in the other room that he'd been able to breathe again.

"No, I'm here," she said foolishly.

"I certainly don't need you cleaning for me. I've got a woman who comes in for that."

"What's her name?"

He stared at her blankly, astonished at the inane conversation they were having. "Hell, I don't know, she's not important; I wouldn't know her if I met her on the street."

Cindy turned around to face the sink and bit her bottom lip at the pain. With slow, deliberate movements, she rinsed out the dishrag and wrung it dry. Patiently, she folded it over the faucet and dried her hands on the kitchen towel.

"Cindy." He touched her shoulder, but she ignored him.

"I promised you I wouldn't leave while you were sleeping," she said, her eyes avoiding his. "But I have to go now. Could I please have the combs?"

"No."

"No?"

"They belonged to your mother, didn't they?"

Cindy nodded.

"Then obviously they mean a great deal to you?"

"Yes...of course." She didn't understand where he was directing the conversation.

"Then I'll keep them until I find out why it's necessary for you to disappear from my life."

Cindy was too shocked to think straight. "That's blackmail."

"I know." He looked pleased with himself. He had her now. "I'll feel a whole lot better once I shower and shave." He ran his hand over the side of his face. "Once I'm finished, we'll talk."

Cindy's fingers gripped the counter behind her. "Okay," she murmured. She hated lying to him, hated misleading him, but she had no intention of staying.

None. She couldn't. She'd kept her promise—she hadn't left while he slept. Now he was awake and so was she. Wide-awake.

The minute she heard the shower running, Cindy sneaked to the bedroom and retrieved her shoes. She was all the way to the front door before she hesitated. A note. He deserved that much.

She found paper and a pen in the kitchen and wrote as fast as her fingers could move. She told him he was right in assuming the combs meant a great deal to her. So much so that she wanted him to keep them in memory of the night they met. She told him she'd always remember him, her own dashing Prince Charming, and that their time together was the most special of her life. Tears filled her eyes and her lips trembled as she signed her name.

She left the paper on top of the television where he was sure to find it. Soundlessly she made her way to the front door. She paused, blinded by tears. Her fingers curled around the knob and she inhaled a wobbly sniffle. Everything within her told her to walk out the door and not look back. Everything that is, except her heart. Cindy felt as if it were dissolving with every breath she drew. She pressed her forehead against the polished mahogany door and cupped her mouth with her hand in an effort to strengthen her resolve.

"I didn't think I could trust you." Thorne said bitterly from behind her.

Chapter Six

Thorne's harsh words cut savagely into Cindy's heart. With tears streaming down her cheeks, she turned to face him, all the pent-up emotion in her eyes there for him to read. He had to see that it was killing her to walk away from him. She was dying by inches.

One look at the pain etched so plainly in her tormented features and Thorne's anger evaporated like dew in the midmorning sun. He moved across the room. "Oh, Cindy," he groaned and reached for her, wrapping her in his arms. At first she resisted his comfort, standing stiff and unyielding against him, but he held her nonetheless because he couldn't bear to let her go. His hands cupped her face and he directed her mouth to his, kissing her again and again until she relaxed and wound her arms around his neck. Thorne could feel her breath quicken and he knew he'd reached her.

Cindy's heart stopped and then surged with quick, liquid fire. Having Thorne hold and kiss her only made leaving him all the more difficult. Yet she couldn't resist him. She could barely breathe past the wild pounding of her heart. She shouldn't have come to him, shouldn't have asked for the return of her mother's combs. But she had—seeking some common ground, praying to forge a trail that would bridge the gap between their lives. Only there was no path, there was no structure to span the Grand Canyon between his wealth and her indomitable pride. His words about his cleaning woman had proven how unfeasible any relationship between them would be.

"No." She eased herself away from him. "Please, don't try to stop me.... I must go."

"But why?"

She pinched her lips together and refused to answer him.

Thorne ran his hand down her thick blond hair to her shoulder. He drew in a calming breath and released it again, repeating the action several times until he could think clearly.

"You're married, aren't you?"

"No." Her denial came hot and fast.

"Then why do you insist upon playing this childish game of hide-and-seek?"

She dropped her head and closed her eyes, unable to look at him any longer. "Trust me, it's for the best that we never see each other again."

"That's ridiculous. We're perfect together." He was nearly shouting at her. He paused and dropped his voice, wanting to reason with her calmly. "I *need* to be with you. That one night was the most wonderful of my life. It was like I'd suddenly woken up from a deep coma. The whole world came alive for me the minute you arrived. At least give us a chance. That isn't so much to ask, is it?''

A tear slipped from the corner of her eye, scorching her face as it rolled down her cheek.

"Cindy, don't you realize I'm crazy about you?"

"You don't know me," she cried.

"I know enough."

"It was one night, don't you see? One magical night. Another could never be the same. It's better to leave things as they are than disillusion ourselves by trying to live a fantasy."

"Cindy." He stopped her, pressing his lips hungrily over hers, kissing her until she was weak and clinging to him. "The magic is stronger than ever. I feel it and so do you. Don't try to deny it."

She leaned her forehead against his chest, battling the resistance her heart was giving her. But she couldn't deny the truth any more than she could stop her heart from racing at his slightest touch.

"One more night," Thorne said softly, enticingly, "to test our feelings. Then we'll know."

Cindy nodded, unable to refuse him anything when he was holding her as if she were an enchanted princess and he were her promised love. Her heart lodged in her throat and when she did speak, her voice was hardly above a whisper. "One more night," she said. "But only one." Any more and it would be impossible to do what she must.

Thorne felt the tightening in his chest subside and the tension seep out of him. He wanted to argue with her; he wanted a lot more than one night—but she looked so confused and uncertain that he didn't dare press her. For now he would be satisfied with the time she could freely give him. Afterward he'd fret, but not now, when she was in his arms.

He grinned. "Where would you like to go? A play? Bobby Short is playing at the Carlyle, and if you haven't heard him, you should. He's fabulous."

"Thorne." Her hand on his arm stopped him. "You're ill."

"I feel a thousand times better." And he did!

"We'll stay right here," she countered, and breaking out of his arms, she strolled into the kitchen. She held Thorne by the hand and dragged him with her. With all the authority of a boot-camp sergeant, she sat him down and proceeded to inspect his freezer and cupboards.

Thorne watched, amazed, as she organized their meal. Before he knew what was happening, Cindy had him at the counter, ripping apart lettuce leaves for a salad. It was as though she'd worked in his kitchen all her life. She located frozen chicken breasts, thawed them in the microwave and placed them in the oven with potatoes wrapped in aluminium foil. Then she searched his cupboards for the ingredients for a mushroom sauce.

Thorne paused long enough in his task to choose a compact disc. Soon music surrounded them as they sat in the living room. Thorne's arm was around her shoulders and she bent her arm to connect her fingers with his. Her head was on his shoulder. Thorne stretched his legs out in front of him and crossed them at the ankles. The moment was serene, peaceful. Thorne had never known a time like this with a woman. Others wanted parties and good times, attention and approval. He hadn't married, hadn't even thought of it until recently. He'd given up looking for that special someone who would fill his days with happiness and love. With Sheila, he'd been willing to accept "close enough," confident he'd never experience what Cindy made so simple. Yet here she was in his arms, and he was willing to do everything humanly possible to keep her there.

Cindy let her head rest on Thorne's shoulder. These few moments together were as close to paradise as she ever hoped to come in this lifetime. She found it astonishing that they didn't need to speak. The communication between them was so strong it didn't require words, and when they did talk, they discovered their tastes were surprisingly similar. Cindy loved to ski, so did Thorne. They'd both read everything Mary Stewart had ever written and devotedly watched reruns of *I Love Lucy*. Both Cindy and Thorne were so familiar with the old black-and-white television comedy that they bounced dialogue off each other, taking on the roles of Lucy and Ricky Ricardo. Excited and happy, they laughed and hugged each other.

Cindy couldn't believe this was happening and held him to her, breathless with an inexplicable joy. Somehow she'd known they'd discover the night of the Christmas Ball hadn't been a fluke.

Thorne couldn't believe how right they were together. Perfect. They loved the same things, shared the same interests. He'd never hoped to find a woman who could make him laugh the way Cindy did.

When dinner was ready, Thorne lit candles, placed them in the center of the dining-room table and dimmed the overhead lighting. The mood was wildly romantic.

"The fairy dust is so thick in here I can barely see," Cindy teased as she delivered their plates to the table.

"That's not fairy dust."

"No?"

"No," he said, and his eyes smiled into hers. "This is undiluted romance." He pulled out her chair for her and playfully nuzzled her neck once she was seated.

"I should have recognized what this is; you'll have to pardon me, but I've been so busy with school that I haven't dated much in the past—" She stopped abruptly, once she realized what she'd said.

Thorne sat down across from her and unfolded the linen napkin. "You attend school?" He'd been so careful not to question her, fearing she'd freeze up on him if he were to bombard her with his need to find answers. From the moment she'd arrived, he'd longed to discover how she'd known he was ill. Cindy was like a complex puzzle. Every tidbit of information he'd learned about her was a tiny interlocking piece that would help him reveal the complete picture of who and what she was—and why she found it so necessary to hide from him.

"I attend classes," she admitted, feeling awkward. Without being obvious, she tried to study his reaction to the information, but his face was an unreadable mask. He'd been in business too long to show his feelings.

"What are you studying?"

"Books." Her stomach tightened and fluttered and she gave him a reproving glance before returning her attention to her meal.

Thorne's grip on his fork tightened as he watched Cindy visibly withdraw from him. Her eyes avoided his, she sat stiff and uneasy in the chair; her mouth was pinched as though she were attempting to disguise her pain. Intuitively he knew that if he continued to press her for answers, he'd lose her completely. "I won't ask you anything more," he promised.

She smiled then and his heart squeezed with an unknown emotion. The ache caught him by surprise. He didn't care who Cindy was. She could be an escaped convict and it wouldn't matter. He wanted to tell her that no matter what it was that troubled her, he could fix it. He'd stand between her and the world if that was what it took. Forging rivers, climbing mountains, anything—he'd do it for her gladly.

After they'd finished eating, Cindy cleared the table. Thorne moved across the living room to change the music.

With tears blinding her, Cindy reached for her coat and purse.

"Do you like easy listening?" Thorne asked without turning. "How about country and western?"

"Anything is fine." Cindy prayed he didn't hear the catch in her voice. She shot him one last look, thanking him with her eyes for the second most magnificent night of her life. Then silently, she slipped out the front door and out of her dreams into the cold harsh world of reality.

"I've got the music to several Broadway shows if you'd prefer that."

His statement was met with silence.

"Cindy?"

He walked into the kitchen. She was gone.

"Cindy?" His voice was hardly audible. He didn't need to look any further. He knew. She'd slipped away when he'd least expected it. Vanished into thin air. He found the note propped on top of the television. She asked him to forgive her. He stared at the words coldly, hating them almost as much as he hated her at that moment.

Thorne folded the paper in half and viciously ripped it, folded it a second time, tore it and folded it again and again until the pieces were impossibly thick. His face went rigid and a muscle worked convulsively in his jaw as he threw her note in the garbage. He stood, furious with her, furious with himself for being caught in this trap a second time.

"Damn you, Cindy," he muttered, and slapped his fist against the counter. "Damn you." He snapped his eyes closed in an effort to control his overpowering anger. Fine, he told himself. If this was the way she wanted it, he'd stay out of her life. Thorndike Prince didn't crawl for any woman—they came to him. His face hardened grimly and his eyes narrowed. He didn't need her. He'd get along perfectly without her and the silly games she wanted to play. He was more determined than ever to put her out of his mind forever. This time he meant it.

Christmas Day was a nightmare for Cindy. She smiled and responded appropriately to what was going on around her, but she was miserable. She couldn't stop thinking about Thorne. She wondered who he was with and what he thought of her... or *if* he did. After the sneaky way she'd left him, Cindy believed he probably hated her. She certainly couldn't blame him.

"Cindy, Cindy..." Her four-year-old cousin crawled into her lap. "Will you read to me?"

Carla had always been special to Cindy. The little girl had been born to Cindy's Aunt Sofia when she was in her early forties. Sofia's three other children were all in their teens and Sofia had been shocked and unhappy about this unexpected pregnancy so late in life. Then Carla had arrived and the child was the delight of the Territo family.

"Mama's busy and all Tony wants to do is talk to Maria."

"Of course, I'll read to you." She gave Carla a squeeze around the middle.

"You're my favorite cousin," Carla whispered close to Cindy's ear.

"I'm glad, because you're my favorite cousin, too," Cindy whispered back. "Now, do you have a book or do you want me to choose one?"

"Santa brought me one."

"Well, good for Santa." Her eye caught her Aunt Sofia's and they exchanged knowing glances. Carla might be only four, but the little girl was well aware that Santa looked amazingly like Uncle Carl, after whom Carla had been named.

"I'll get it," Carla crawled off Cindy's lap, raced across the room and returned a minute later with a wide grin. "Here," she said and handed the large picture book to Cindy. "Read me this one. Read me 'Cinderella.'"

Cindy's breath jammed in her lungs and the brimming tears stung her eyes. "'Cinderella'?" she repeated as the numbing sensation worked its way over her body. She prayed it would anesthetize her from the trauma that gripped her heart.

"Cindy?" Carla's chubby little hands shook Cindy's knee. "Aren't you going to read to me?"

"Of course, sweetheart." Somehow she managed to pick up the book and flip open the front cover. Carla positioned herself comfortably in her cousin's lap, leaned back and promptly inserted her thumb in her mouth.

It demanded all Cindy's energy to open her lips and start reading. Her throat felt incredibly dry. "'Once upon a time...'"

"...in a land far away," Mary Susan Clark told her five-year-old son, who sat on the brocade cushion at her feet.

Thorne's gaze rested on his sister, who was reciting the fairy tale to her son, and his heart rate slowed with anger and resentment. "Do you think it's such a good idea to be filling a young boy's head with that kind of garbage?" Thorne demanded gruffly.

Mary Susan's gray eyes widened with surprise. "But it's only a fairy tale."

"Thorne." His mother's puzzled gaze studied his. "It's not like you to snap."

"I apologize," he said with a weak smile. "I guess I have been a bit short-tempered lately."

"You've been ill." Sheila, with her dark brown eyes and pixie face, automatically defended him. She placed her hand in his and gave his fingers a gentle squeeze.

Sheila was a nice girl, Thorne mused: pleasant and loyal. Someday she'd make a man an excellent wife. Maybe even him. Thorne was through playing Cindy's

games. Through believing in fairy tales. He couldn't
live like this. Cindy didn't want to have anything to do
with him, and he had no choice but to accept her
wishes. Sheila loved him—at least she claimed she did.
Thorne didn't know what love felt like anymore. At
one time he'd thought he was in love with Sheila.
Maybe not completely, but he'd expected that emotion to come in time. Then he'd met Cindy, and he was
head over heels in love for the first time in his thirty-
three years. Overnight, he'd been hooked. Crazy in
love. And with a woman who'd turned her back on him
and walked away without a second thought. It didn't
make sense. Nothing did anymore. Nothing at all. Not
business. Not life. Not women.

Thorne and Sheila had been seeing each other for
nearly six months and Thorne knew she'd hardly been
able to conceal her disappointment when an engagement ring hadn't been secretly tucked under the
Christmas tree. But she hadn't questioned him. He
wished she wasn't so damned understanding; he'd have
liked her better if she'd gotten angry and demanded an
explanation.

Thorne noticed his mother studying him and he
made an effort to disguise his discontent. Smiling required a monumental effort. He managed it, but he
sincerely doubted that he'd fooled his mother.

"Thorne, could you help me in the kitchen?"

The whole family turned their attention to him. The
old ploy for talking privately wasn't the least bit origi-
nal.

"Of course, Mother," he said with the faintest sardonic inflection. He disentangled his fingers from

Sheila's and stood, obediently following Gwendolyn Prince out of the room.

"What in heaven's name is the matter with you?" she demanded, the minute they were out of earshot. "It isn't that...that girl you mentioned, is it?"

"What girl?" Feigning ignorance seemed the best possible response.

"You haven't been yourself..."

"Since the night of that Christmas Ball," Cindy's Aunt Theresa said softly.

The silence that followed grated on Cindy's frayed nerves. "I know," she whispered. "You see, there's something I didn't know...fairy tales don't always come true."

"But, Cindy, you're eating your heart out over him."

"We said goodbye," she answered, her eyes pleading with her aunt to drop this disturbing subject. Accepting that she would live her life without Thorne was difficult enough; rehashing it with her aunt was like tearing open a half-healed wound.

"But you haven't stopped thinking about him."

"No, but I will in time."

"Will you, Cindy?" Theresa's deep brown eyes revealed her doubt.

Her gaze pleaded with the older woman's. "Yes," she said and the words were a vow to herself. She had no choice now. When she'd left Thorne's apartment it had been forever. Although the pain had been nearly unbearable, it was better to sever the ties quickly and sharply than to bleed to death slowly.

* * *

"Mother and I are planning a shopping expedition to Paris in March," Sheila spoke enthusiastically, sitting across the green table from Thorne.

They were at one of Thorne's favorite lunch spots. Sheila had made it a habit to drop by unexpectedly at the office at least once a week so they could have lunch. In the past, Thorne had looked forward to their get-togethers. Not today. He wasn't in the mood. But before he'd been able to say anything to Mrs. Hillard, she'd sent Sheila into his office, and now he was stuck.

"Paris sounds interesting."

"So does the chicken," Sheila commented, glancing over the menu. "I hear the mushroom sauce here is fabulous."

Thorne's stomach clenched violently. "Baked chicken breast served with mushroom sauce," he repeated, remembering all too well his last evening with Cindy and the meal she'd prepared for him.

"I hope you'll try it with me," Sheila urged, gazing adoringly at him.

Thorne's mouth thinned. "I hate mushrooms."

Sheila's gaze dropped again to the menu and she pressed her lips tightly together. "I didn't know that," she said after a long minute.

"You do now," Thorne snapped, detesting himself for treating her this way. Sheila deserved better.

The waiter stepped to the table, his hands clenched behind his back, and he smiled down on them cordially. "Are you ready to order?"

"I believe so," Thorne said, closing his menu and handing it to the other man. "The lady will have the chicken special and I'll have a mushroom omelet."

Sheila gave him an odd look, but said nothing.

During lunch Thorne made a sincere effort to be pleasant. He honestly tried to appear interested when Sheila told him about the latest trends in fashion she hoped to wear once she returned from France. He even managed to stifle a yawn when she hinted at the possibility of buying several yards of exclusive French lace. It wasn't until they'd left the restaurant and were walking toward his office that Thorne caught the implication. French lace—wedding gown.

"And I was thinking..."

Sheila's voice faded and Thorne quickened his pace. There. The blonde, half a block ahead of him. Cindy. Dear God, it was Cindy.

"Thorne," Sheila announced breathlessly. "You're walking so fast, I can't keep up with you."

Without thought, he brushed her arm from his. "Excuse me a minute." He didn't remove his gaze from Cindy, fearing he'd lose her in the heavy holiday crowds.

"Thorne?"

He ignored Sheila and took off running, weaving in and around the moving bodies that filled the sidewalk on the Avenue of the Americas.

"Cindy!" He yelled her name, but either she didn't hear or else she was trying to escape him. Again. He wouldn't let her. He'd found her now. Relief flowed through him and he savored the sweet taste of it. He had dreamed something like this would happen. Somehow, some way he'd miraculously stumble upon her. Every time he stepped out of his apartment, he found himself studying faces, looking. Seeking. Searching for her in a silent quest that dominated his every waking thought. And now she was only a few feet from him, her brisk pace no match for his easy sprint. Her blond hair swished back and forth, hitting the top of her shoulders. Her dark navy wool coat was wrapped securely around her.

Sharply Thorne raced around two couples, cutting abruptly in front of them. He didn't know what he'd do first: kiss her or shake her until she begged him to stop. Kiss her, he decided.

"Cindy." He caught up with her finally and placed his hand on her shoulder.

"I beg your pardon." The woman, over fifty, shouted and slapped his hand away. She didn't even resemble Cindy. She was older, plain, and embarrassed by his attention.

Thorne blinked back the disbelief. "I thought you were someone else."

"Obviously. Mind your manners, young man, or I'll report you to the police."

"I apologize." He couldn't move. His feet felt rooted to the sidewalk and his arms hung lifelessly at his sides. Cindy was driving him mad; he was slowly but surely losing his mind a minute at a time.

"Decent women aren't safe in this city anymore," the woman grumbled and quickly stepped away.

"Thorne! Thorne!" Sheila joined him, her hands gripping his arm. "Who was she?"

"No one." He couldn't stop looking at the blonde as she made her way down the street. He would have sworn it was Cindy. He would have wagered a year's salary that the woman who couldn't escape him fast enough had been Cindy. His Cindy. His love.

"Thorne," Sheila droned, patting his hand. "You've been working too hard. I'm worried about you."

"I'm fine," he snapped. "Just fine."

The pinched look returned to Sheila's face, but she didn't argue. "March gives you plenty of time to arrange a vacation. We'll have a marvelous time in Paris. I'll take you shopping with me and let you pick out my trousseau."

"I'm not going to Paris," he barked.

Sheila continued to pat his hand. "I do wish you'd consider it, Thorne. You haven't been yourself lately. Not at all."

He couldn't agree more.

Two hours later Thorne sat at his desk reading over the financial statements the accounting department had sent up for him to approve.

"Mr. Williams is here," his secretary informed him.

Instantly Thorne closed the folder. "Send him in."

"Right away," Mrs. Hillard returned crisply.

Thorne stood to greet the balding man with a wide space between his two front teeth. He wore a suit that looked as if it hadn't been dry-cleaned since it came off the rack at Sears ten years before. His potbelly gave credence to the claim that Mike Williams was the best private detective in the business: from the looks of it, he ate well enough.

"Mr. Williams," Thorne said, extending his hand to the other man.

They exchanged brisk handshakes. The man's grip was solid. Thorne approved.

"What can I do for you?"

Thorne motioned toward the chair and Mike sat.

"I want you to find someone for me," Thorne said, without preamble.

Mike nodded. "It's what I do best. What's the name?"

Thorne reclaimed his chair and his hands gripped the armrest as he leaned back, giving an impression of indifference. This wasn't going to be easy, but he hadn't expected it would be. "Cindy."

"Anything else?" The detective reached for his pencil and pad.

"I'm not completely sure that's her name. It could have been contrived." Thorne was braced to accept anything where Cindy was concerned. Everything and anything.

"Where did you meet her?"

"At a party. The one put on by this company—she doesn't work here, I've already checked."

Williams nodded.

"She did leave these behind." Thorne leaned forward to hand the detective one pearl comb. "But I've had it appraised and the comb isn't uncommon. She claimed they belonged to her mother. There are no markings that would distinguish them from ten thousand identical combs."

Again Williams nodded, but he carefully examined the comb. "Can I take this?" he asked and stuck it in his pocket.

Thorne agreed with a swift nod of his head. "I'll want it back."

"Of course."

They spoke for an additional fifteen minutes and Thorne recalled with as much clarity as possible every meeting with Cindy.

Williams stopped him only once. "A limo, you said."

"Yes." Thorne scooted forward in his chair. He'd forgotten that. Cindy had gotten into a limousine that first night when she'd escaped from him. She'd handed him his coat, run across the street and immediately been met by a long black limousine.

"You wouldn't happen to remember the license plate, would you?"

"No." Disgustedly, Thorne shook his head. "I'm afraid I can't."

"Don't worry about it. I have enough." Williams briefly scanned the details he'd listed and flipped the pad closed. Slowly, he came to his feet.

"Can you find her?" Thorne stood as well.

"I'll give it my best shot."

"Good." Thorne hoped the man couldn't see how desperate he'd become.

A cold northern wind bit into Cindy's arms as she waited on the sidewalk outside the Oakes-Jenning building well past midnight. She was exhausted—both physically and mentally. She hadn't been sleeping well and the paper she should be writing during the holiday break just wouldn't come, although she'd done all the required research. It was Thorne. No matter what she did, she couldn't stop thinking about him.

Her Uncle Sal pulled to a stop at the curb. Cindy stepped away from the building and scooted inside to the front seat beside him.

"Hi," she greeted, forcing a smile. Her family was worried about her and Cindy did her best to ease their fears; she'd be fine, given time.

"A private detective was poking around the house today," her uncle announced, starting into the traffic. Cindy felt her heart go cold. "What did he want?"

"He was asking about you."

Chapter Seven

Asking about me... What did you tell him?''

"Not a damn thing."

"But..."

"He wanted to look at my appointment schedule for December 15, but I wouldn't let him."

The chilly sensation that had settled over Cindy dropped below freezing. Her uncle's refusal would only create suspicions. The detective would be back, and there would be more questions Sal would refuse to answer. The detective wouldn't accept that, and he'd return again and again until he had the information he wanted. This stranger would make trouble for her family. Cindy could see it as clearly as if it were printed across the sky in huge, bold strokes. In a hundred years, she would never have guessed that Thorne would go to such lengths to locate her. She had to find a way to stop him…a way to make him understand and leave things as they were.

Cindy went to bed thinking about the situation and arose more tired and troubled than she was before she'd slept. Repeatedly she examined her own role in this rash venture. Playing the part of Cinderella for one night had seemed so innocent, so adventurous, so exciting. She'd slipped into the fantasy with uncanny ease, but the night had ended with the stroke of midnight and she could never go back to being a fairy-tale figure again. She'd let go of the illusion and yes, it had been painful, but she'd been given no choice. The consequences of that one foolhardy night would follow her all the days of her life.

She had never dreamed it would be possible to feel as strongly about a man in so short a time as she did about Thorne. But the emotion wasn't based on any of the usual prerequisites for love. It couldn't be. They had only seen each other twice.

Thorne might believe he felt as strongly about her, Cindy realized as her thoughts rambled on, but that wasn't real either. She was a challenge: the mystery woman who had briefly touched his life. Once he learned the truth and realized she'd made a fool of him, it would be over. Given no other option, Cindy realized she'd have to tell Thorne who she really was.

"He could fire me," she said aloud several soul-searching hours later. Her hands clenched her purse protectively under her arm as she stood outside the Oakes-Jenning Financial Services building. Employees streamed out in a steady flow. Cindy stood against the side of the building, back just far enough to examine their faces as they made their way out the heavy glass doors. They all looked so serious, somber and grave. Cindy didn't know much about the business world, but it certainly seemed to employ dour souls. Thorne included.

For most of the afternoon, Cindy had weighed the possible consequences of telling Thorne the truth. Losing her job was only one of several unpleasant options that had crossed her mind. And ultimately he could hate her, which would be so much worse than anything else he could do to her. She wanted to scream at him for being so obstinate, so willful, so determined to force himself into her life. He had to know that she didn't want to be found, and yet he'd ignored her wishes and driven her to this. He'd forced her into doing the one thing she dreaded most: telling him the truth.

Her tenacity hardened as she watched Thorne step outside the building, his face as staid as the others. He carried a briefcase in his hand and walked briskly past her. Unseeing. Uncaring. As oblivious to her then as he was every morning when he walked into his clean office.

"Thorne." She didn't shout, her voice was little more than a whisper.

Abruptly he stopped, almost in midstride, and turned around. "Cindy?" His gaze scanned the sea of faces that swam before him. "Cindy?" he repeated, louder this time, uncertain if this was real. He'd been half out of his mind for days on end. Nothing shocked him anymore. He'd recognized her voice instantly, but that too could be part of his deep yearning to find her. She was here and she'd called to him, and he'd uproot this sidewalk before he'd let her escape him again.

"Here." She took a step closer, her hands clenched into hard fists at her side. "Call off the detective. I'll tell you—" She wasn't allowed to finish.

Thorne dropped the briefcase onto the cement, gripped her shoulders and roughly hauled her into his arms. His mouth came down on hers with such force that he drove the breath from her lungs. His hand dug into her hair as he tangled the thick blond tresses with his fingers, as though binding her to him for all time. His mouth slanted over hers and left her in little doubt regarding the strength of his emotions.

Cindy's first reaction was stunned surprise. Her hands hung uselessly at her sides. She'd expected him to be furious, to shout at her and demand an explanation. But not this. Never this.

Once the initial shock of his kiss faded, she surrendered to the sheer pleasure of simply being in his arms. She held on to him, wrapping her arms around him, relishing the rush of sensations that came springing up from within her like the profusion of flowers that follows a spring rain. She couldn't have pushed him away had her life depended on it. The rock-hard resolution to ruthlessly end their nonrelationship had melted the minute he'd reached for her.

"This had better not be a dream," Thorne said, moving his lips against her temple. "You taste so unbelievably real."

Cindy flattened her palms against his chest in an effort to break away, but he held her steadfast. "Thorne, please, people are looking."

"Let them." He kissed her again, with such hunger and greed that she was left breathless and utterly boggled. Disoriented, she made a weak effort to break loose of his grip, but Thorne had backed her against the side of the building and there was nowhere to move. And even if there had been, she was convinced he wouldn't have released her.

"Thorne," she pleaded. Every second he continued to hold her ate up her determination to explain everything. He felt so warm and vital...so wonderful. "Please...don't," she begged as he covered her face with kisses. Even as she was speaking, pleading with him to stop, she was turning her head one way and then another to grant him freedom to do as he wished.

"I'm starving for you," he said before feasting on her mouth one more time.

"Please." The sob worked its way up her windpipe. She was so weak-willed with Thorne. She could start out with the firmest of resolves but ten seconds after being with him, she had all the fortitude of a roasted marshmallow.

"Cindy, dear God—" his arms tightened "—I've been crazy these past few days without you."

The time hadn't been any less traumatic for Cindy. "You hired a detective?"

"He found you?"

"No...I heard you were looking." Lovingly her hands framed his face. "Thorne, please call him off." She viewed the private detective as a dog nipping at her heels. An irritant who had the power to turn her life upside down and intimidate those she loved most. "I'll tell you everything you want to know...only, please, please, don't hate me."

"Hate you?" His look was incredulous. "It isn't in me to feel any different than I did the night we met." For the first time he seemed to notice the stares they were generating. "Let's get out of here." He reached for her hand and marched her purposefully away.

"Thorne," she cried, tossing a surprised glance over her shoulder. "Your briefcase."

He looked so utterly astonished that he could have forgotten it, Cindy laughed outright.

Without hesitating, he turned and went back to retrieve it, dragging her with him. "Do you see what you do to me?" His words were clipped, almost angry.

"Do you know what you do to me?" she returned with equal consternation.

"I must have one hell of an effect on you, all right. You can't seem to get away from me fast enough. You sneak away like a thief in the night and turn up when I least expect it. I don't sleep well, my appetite is gone and I'm convinced you're playing me for a fool."

"Oh, Thorne, you don't honestly believe that, do you?" She came to an abrupt stop. People walked a large circle around them, but Cindy wasn't concerned. She couldn't bear it if Thorne believed anything less than what she truly felt for him. "I think I'd rather die than let you assume for one minute that I didn't care for you."

"You have one hell of a way of showing it."

"But, Thorne, if you'd stop and give me time to—"

Undaunted by the traffic, Thorne paraded them halfway into the street, his arm raised. "Taxi!"

"Where are we going?"

A yellow cab pulled up in front of them. Thorne ignored her question as his hand bit unmercifully into her elbow. He opened the car door for her and climbed in beside her a second later.

Before Cindy had an opportunity to speak, Thorne draped his elbow over the front seat and spoke to the driver. When he'd finished he leaned back and stared at her as though he still weren't completely convinced she wasn't a ghostly illusion.

Cindy didn't know what she'd expected. She hadn't thought about where she'd talk to Thorne, only that she would. Over and over she'd rehearsed what she wanted to say. But she hadn't counted on him hauling her halfway across Manhattan to some unknown destination. From the looks he was giving her now, he didn't appear any too pleased with finding her.

Thorne relaxed against the cushion and expelled a long sigh. "Do you realize we've been to bed together and I don't even know your name?"

Cindy felt more than saw the driver's interest perk up. Color exploded into her cheeks as she glared hotly at Thorne. "Would you kindly stop?" she hissed. He was doing this on purpose, to punish her.

"I don't think I can." He regarded her levelly. "Look at me! I'm shaking like a leaf. You've got me so twisted up inside, I don't know what's real and what's not anymore. My parents think I need to see a shrink and I'm beginning to agree with them!"

Cindy covered his hand with her own. "I'm certainly not anything like the Cinderella you met that night." Her voice was a raw whisper, filled with pain. "I thought I could pretend to be something I'm not for one glamorous night, but it's all backfired. I've hated deceiving you—you deserve better than me."

"Is your name really Cindy?"

She nodded. "That's what started it all. Now I wish I'd been named something like Hermione or Frieda—

anything but Cindy. If I had, then maybe, just maybe I wouldn't have believed in that night and decided to do something so stupid.''

"No matter who you are and what you've done," Thorne told her solemnly, "I'll never regret the Christmas Ball."

"That's the problem—I can't either. I'll treasure it always. But Thorne, don't you see? I'm not Cinderella; I'm only me."

"In case you haven't noticed, I'm not exactly Prince Charming."

"But you are," Cindy argued.

"No. And that's been our problem all along; we each seemed to think the other wanted to continue the fantasy." He placed his arm around her and drew her close to his side. "That one evening was marvelous, but it was one night in a million. If we're to develop a relationship, it has to be between the people we are now."

Cindy leaned against him, sighed inwardly and closed her eyes as he rubbed his chin across the top of her head.

"I want to continue being with Cindy," he said tenderly, "not the imaginary Cinderella."

"But Cindy will disappoint you."

"If you're looking for Prince Charming in me, then I fear you're in for a sad awakening as well."

"You don't even know who I am."

"It doesn't matter." Her sweet face commanded all his attention. He read her lovely blue eyes as easily as a child's reader. Something deep inside her was insecure and frightened. She'd bolted and run away from him twice, her doubts overtaking her. No more. Whatever Williams had dug up about her had worked.

She was here because he'd gotten close to her, close enough to bring her back to him.

She really was a lovely creature. Gentle and good. Beautiful in ways that stirred his heart. Her eyes were wide and inquiring, her lips moist from his recent kisses. He'd found his Cindy and could on go with his life again. The restless feeling that had eaten at him these past few days was dissipating every moment he spent with her. He was a man who liked his privacy, and overnight he'd discovered he was lonely and couldn't adjust to the solitude. Not when he'd found the one woman he meant to share his world with. All he had to do was convince her of that. Only this time, he'd be more cautious. He wouldn't make demands of her. She could tell him whatever was troubling her when she was ready. Every time he started questioning her, it ended in disaster.

Cindy sat upright, holding her back stiff as she turned her head and glanced out the side window. He was right. They couldn't go back to the night of the Christmas Ball. But she wasn't completely convinced they could form a compatible relationship as Thorne and Cindy.

"You say it doesn't matter now," she said thoughtfully, "but when I tell you that I'm the girl who—"

"Stop." His hand reached for hers, squeezing her fingers tightly. "Are you married, engaged or currently involved with another man?"

She twisted around and glared at him for even suggesting such a thing. "No, of course not."

"Involved in any illegal activity?"

She scooted several inches away from him and sat starchly erect, shocked that his questions could pain her heart so. Her brow knitted with consternation. "Is that what you think?"

"Just answer the question."

"No." The lone word had difficulty making it up her throat. She looped a thick strand of honey-colored hair around her ear in nervous agitation. "I don't cheat, rarely lie and am disgustingly law-abiding—I don't even jaywalk, and in New York that's something!"

Thorne's warm smile chased the chill from her bones. "Then who and what you are is of no importance. You're the one who seems to be filled with objections. What I feel for you appears to be of little consequence."

"That's not true, I'm only trying to save you from embarrassment."

"Embarrassment?"

"My family name isn't linked with three generations of banking."

"I wouldn't care if it was linked with garbage collecting."

"You think that now," she snapped. He didn't realize how close he was to the truth!

"I mean that. I'm falling in love with a girl named Cindy, not a fairy-tale figure who magically appeared in my life. She's wonderfully bright and funny and loving."

Falling in love with her! Cindy's heart felt like it was going to burst with happiness just hearing him suggest such a marvelous thing. Then she realized the impossibility of a lasting relationship between them. Dejectedly she lowered her gaze. "Please don't say that."

"What? That I'm falling in love with you?"

"Yes."

"It's true. All I know is that you've been driving me insane the past few weeks. How can I know what I really feel if you keep jumping in and out of my life?"

"But you hardly know me," she cried. Yet it hadn't deterred her from falling head over heels for him.

The taxi came to a stop in the heavy traffic. The driver placed his hand along the back of the seat and twisted around. "Central Park is on your left."

"Central Park?" Cindy echoed, pleased at his choice of locations to do their talking.

"I thought we should return here and start over again." He diverted his attention for the moment while handing the driver several crisp dollar bills. A moment later, he joined Cindy on the sidewalk. He tucked her hand in the crook of his arm and smiled seductively down on her.

Her returning smile was feeble at best.

"Hello, there," he said softly. "I'm Thorne, which is short for Thorndike, which was my father's name and his father's before him."

"I'm a first-generation Cindy."

"Well, Cindy, now that we've been properly introduced, will you have dinner with me tonight?"

"I...can't." She hated to refuse him, but she couldn't spend time with him when she was paid to clean his office. As it was, she was due there within the half hour.

His face tightened briefly. "Can't or won't?"

"Can't." Regret weighted the lone word.

"Tomorrow, then."

"But it's New Year's Eve." Surely he had other places to go, and far more important people to spend the evening with than she. Arguments filled her head and were dispelled with one enticing look from Thorne.

"New Year's Eve or not, I'll pick you up and we'll paint the town." He felt Cindy tense and understood why. Quickly he amended his offer. "All right, I'll meet you somewhere. Anyplace you say."

"In front of Oakes-Jenning." Although it was a holiday, she would be working; she couldn't afford to turn down time and a half. "I . . . won't be available until after eleven-thirty."

"Fine, I'll be there."

"You're late," Vanessa informed Cindy unnecessarily, when she ran breathlessly into the basement supply room.

"I know."

"Where were you?"

"Central Park." Her hands made busy work filling her cart with the needed supplies. She'd left after promising Thorne she would meet him the following night. His gaze had pleaded with her to give him something to hold on to—a phone number, a name, anything. But Cindy had given him something of far more value: her word. Letting her go had been a measure of his trust. She could see that he wasn't pleased, but he hadn't drilled her with questions or made any other demands on her.

What he'd said made sense. Neither one of them could continue playing the role of someone they weren't. Cinderella was now Cindy and Prince Charming had gone back to being Thorne. They'd been a bit awkward with each other at first, but gradually that uneasiness had evaporated and they'd quickly become friends.

Cindy was beginning to believe that although there were plenty of obstacles blocking their paths, together they could possibly overcome them. There hadn't been much time to say the things she must because Cindy had been forced to rush to work. She hadn't explained that to Thorne, and watched as a jealous anger marred his face.

"What are you thinking?" Vanessa asked her, studying her friend.

"Nothing."

"Nothing," her friend complained. "Oh, good grief, are we back to that?"

Cindy relented. "I'm seeing Thorne tomorrow night."

"You are?" Even Vanessa sounded shocked. "But it's New Year's Eve...oh, heavens, girl, did you forget we have to work?"

"No...I told him I wouldn't be ready until after eleven-thirty."

"And he didn't ask for any explanation?"

"Not really." The questions had been there, his eyes had been filled with them, but he hadn't voiced a single one. Cindy felt her friend regarding her thoughtfully and made busywork around the cart, taking the items she needed before heading for the upper floor.

Oh, Lord, she only hoped she was doing the right thing. Thorne kept insisting that who she was didn't matter to him. She was going to test that and in the process wager her heart and her happiness.

"Thorne, it's your mother."

Thorne frowned into the telephone receiver. He could tell by the slight edge to her voice that she was going to bring up an unpleasant subject: Sheila. The other woman was quickly becoming a thorn in his side.

"Yes, Mother," he returned obediently.

"Your father and I are having a New Year's Eve party tomorrow night and we'd like you to attend."

Parties had never been his forte, which was one of the reasons his mother had been so keen on Sheila, who loved to socialize. Sheila would be good for his career, his father had once told him. At the time, Thorne had considered that an important factor in choosing a wife. Not anymore.

"I apologize, Mother, but I'll have to decline, I've already made plans."

"But, Sheila said—"

"I won't be with Sheila," he responded shortly.

"Oh, dear, is it that Cheryl woman again? I'd thought that was over."

"Cindy," he corrected, swallowing a laugh. He knew his mother too well. She remembered Cindy's name as well as she did her own.

"I see." His mother returned, her voice sharpening with disapproval. "Then you haven't said anything to Sheila."

"As I recall, you advised me against it," he reminded her.

"But, Thorne, the dear girl is beside herself with worry. And what's this about you chasing a strange woman down some sidewalk? Really, Thorne, what has gotten into you?"

"I'm in love."

The shocked silence that followed his announcement nearly made him laugh right into the phone. His
parents had been waiting years for him to announce
that he'd chosen a wife, and now that he was in love,
one would think he'd committed a terrible crime.
However, Thorne was convinced that once his parents
met Cindy, they'd understand, and love her, too.

"Are you claiming to love a woman you hardly
know?"

"That's right, Mother."

"What about her family?"

"What about them?"

"Thorne!"

His mother sounded aghast, which only increased
Thorne's amusement. "You'd feel better if you could
meet her?"

"I'm not sure . . . I suppose it would help."

"Dinner, then, the first part of next week. I'll clear
it with Cindy and get back to you."

"Fine." But she didn't sound enthusiastic. "In the
meantime, would you talk to Sheila? She hasn't heard
from you all week."

"What do you suggest I say to her?"

"Tell her . . . tell her you need a few days to think
things through. That should appease her for now. Once
I've had a chance to . . . meet your Cheryl, I'll have a
better feel for the situation."

"Yes, Mother," he said obediently and replaced the
receiver. Family had always been important to Thorne,
but he wouldn't allow his mother or any other family
member to rule his life.

Leaning back, Thorne folded his arms behind his
head. He felt good, wonderful. He'd never looked

forward more to a night in his life. New Year's Eve with Cindy. And with it the promise of spending every year with her for the rest of his life.

The following day, Thorne only worked until noon. He did some errands, ate a light dinner around six, showered and dressed casually. The television killed time, but he discovered he couldn't keep his eyes off the wall clock. He'd leave around eleven, he'd figured. That would give him plenty of time to get to Oakes-Jenning, and from there he'd take Cindy to Times Square. It was something he'd always wanted to do, but had never had the chance. They could lose themselves in the crowd and he'd have every excuse to keep her close.

The doorbell chimed around eight, and Thorne hurried for the front door, convinced it was Cindy. Somehow, some way, she'd come to him early. His excitement died an untimely death when he found Sheila standing in the outside hallway.

"Sheila."

"Hello, Thorne." She glanced up at him through seductively thick lashes. "May I come in?"

He stepped aside. "Sure."

"You're looking delightfully casual." She entered the apartment, removed her coat, sat on the sofa and crossed her legs.

"This is a surprise." He stood awkwardly in the center of the room and buried his hands in his pockets.

"I haven't heard from you since our luncheon date and thought I'd stop in unannounced. I hope you don't mind?"

Thorne would have preferred to choose another day, but since she'd come, there was probably no better time than the present to tell her about Cindy. "I'm glad you did." At the light of happiness that flashed in her eyes, Thorne regretted his poor choice of words.

She folded her hands in her lap and regarded him with such adoration that Thorne felt his stomach knot.

"Sometimes I do such a terrible job of explaining my feelings," she said softly and lowered her gaze to her hands. She smoothed out a wrinkle on the thigh of her purple satin jumpsuit and released a soft, feminine sigh. "I want you to know how very much you mean to me."

The knot in Thorne's stomach worked its way to his chest, painfully tightening it. "I treasure your friendship as well."

She arched her pencil-thin brows. "I thought we were so much more than simply friends."

Thorne claimed the ottoman and scooted it so that he sat directly in front of her. "This isn't easy, Sheila."

"Don't." She stopped him. "I already know what you're going to say.... You've met someone else."

"I don't want to hurt you." They had been seeing each other steadily for months, and although he realized how mismatched they were, Sheila hadn't seen it yet, and he honestly wished to spare her any emotional pain.

"But you see, darling you don't need to. I understand about these things."

"You do?" Thorne hadn't the foggiest notion what there was for her to understand.

"A woman must accept this sort of thing from her husband. I know Daddy's had his women on the side. Mother knows and approves."

Thorne surged to his feet. "You're saying you expect me to have an affair?"

"Just to get her out of your system. I want you to know that I understand."

Years of discipline tempered Thorne's response. He was so furious that it took all his restraint to continue being civil, following Sheila's generous announcement. He marched to the plate-glass window and looked out, afraid to speak for fear of what he'd say. Instead he analyzed his anger.

"Thorne, you look upset."

"I am." He realized he was so outraged because Sheila's seeming generosity had subtly insulted Cindy by suggesting she belonged on some back street.

"But, why?"

"Cindy isn't that kind of woman," he said, and turned around. "And neither are you."

A gust of feminine tears followed. Embarrassed, Thorne retrieved a box of tissues and held Sheila gently in his arms until she'd finished weeping.

Dabbing her eyes, Sheila announced that she needed something to drink and nodded approvingly when Thorne brought out a bottle of expensive French wine he knew she enjoyed. He had plenty of time to soothe her wounded ego. Cindy wouldn't be available until almost midnight.

Once Sheila had dried her eyes, she was good company, chatting about the fun times they'd shared over the months they'd been seeing each other and getting slightly tipsy in the process.

Slowly, Thorne felt his anger evaporate. Sheila did most of the talking, and when she suggested they have a cocktail at the Carlyle, Thorne agreed. It was hours before he could meet Cindy.

The Carlyle was crowded, as were two of Sheila's other favorite hangouts where they stopped for drinks.

"Let's drop by at your parents'," she suggested casually, swirling the ice in her empty glass.

"I can't, I'm meeting Cindy in a couple of hours." He raised his arm to look at his watch and the air left his lungs in one disbelieving gasp. "I'm late."

"But, Thorne..."

It was already eleven forty-five and he was at least another fifteen minutes from Oakes-Jenning. The regret seared through him like a hot coal.

"You can't just leave me here!" Sheila cried, trotting after him.

He handed the stub to the hatcheck girl and paced restlessly until she returned. When she did, Thorne thrust the girl a generous tip for being prompt.

"Thorne." Sheila gave him a forlorn look, her eyes damp with tears. "Don't leave me."

Chapter Eight

All New York seemed alive with activity to Cindy. New Year's Eve and it could have been noon for all the people milling in the streets. Times Square would already be a madhouse, filled with anxious spectators waiting for the magical hour when the Big Apple would descend, marking the beginning of another New Year.

Cindy felt wonderful. Free. Thorne might have claimed not to be Prince Charming, but he'd demonstrated several princely qualities. From the way he'd searched for her, he seemed to hold a deep, genuine affection for her. Surely he wouldn't have hired a private detective to find her if he didn't care. Nor would he have been satisfied with the cloak of secrecy she wore like a heavy shroud. He wasn't pleased with the way she kept magically popping in and out of his life, but he accepted it. He claimed it didn't matter who or what she was, and to prove his point he'd refused to listen when she'd yearned to explain everything. He didn't demand answers when the questions were clearly etched in his eyes, nor did he make any unreasonable demands of her. She'd told him she couldn't meet him until eleven-thirty, and without voicing any qualms he'd accepted that.

A police car, with its siren screaming, raced down the street and Cindy watched its progress. A glance at her watch told her Thorne was fifteen minutes late. After months of cleaning up after Thorne, Cindy would confidently say that he was rarely tardy for anything. He was too much the business tycoon to be unaware of the clock.

Remembering the police car, Cindy stepped to the curb and looked up and down the street. Unexpectedly, alarm filled her. Perhaps something had happened to Thorne. Perhaps he was hurt and bleeding—maybe he'd suffered a relapse and was ill again.

Cindy couldn't bear to think of him in pain. She'd rather endure it herself than have him suffer. It took her another five minutes to reason things out. Thorne was perfectly capable of taking care of himself, and she was worrying needlessly. He'd gotten hung up in traffic and would arrive any minute. If he was hurt, she'd know. Somehow, some way, her heart would know. By fair means or foul, Thorne would come to her, no matter what the circumstances. All she had to do was be patient and wait. He couldn't look at her the way he did and ask her to spend this night with him and then leave her standing in the cold. She'd stake her life on it.

Thirty minutes later, Cindy's confidence was dying a slow, painful death. She was cold. Her face felt frozen and her toes were numb. She'd been silly enough to wear open-toed pumps and was paying the price of her own folly. She hunched her shoulders against the cutting cold as the wind whipped her hair back and forth across her face. Resentfully she thought of how hard she'd worked, rushing from one office to another to finish in record time, and how quickly she'd showered and changed clothes all so she could spend extra time with her hair and makeup. She'd wanted this night to be perfect for Thorne. After forty-five minutes of standing in the wind, her hair was a lost cause and her makeup couldn't have fared any better.

Another fifteen minutes, Cindy decided. That was all the time she'd give him.

And then fifteen intolerable, interminable minutes passed.

Five more, she vowed, and that was it. She'd walk away and not look back. Thorne would have a logical explanation, she was convinced of that, but she couldn't stand in the cold all night or she'd freeze to death.

Dejected, discouraged and defeated, Cindy waited out the allotted five minutes and decided there was nothing more she could do but leave. Tucking her coat more securely around her, she walked to the corner and paused. Not yet. She couldn't leave yet. What if Thorne arrived and they just missed each other? She couldn't bear for him to find her gone. He'd be frantic.

She pulled her hand from her pocket and examined her watch one last time. Maybe she should wait another minute or two—it wouldn't hurt anything. Her toes were beyond feeling and a couple more minutes wouldn't matter.

A niggling voice in the back of her mind tried to convince her that Thorne had left her waiting in the cold as just punishment for brusquely disrupting his staid, regimented life.

Forcefully, Cindy shook her head. She refused to believe it. The voice returned a moment later and suggested that Thorne was with another woman. Sheila. This possibility seemed far more feasible. The photograph of the other woman remained on prominent display in his office. A hundred doubts crowded each other as they battled for space in her troubled thoughts. Sheila. He was with Sheila!

Determined now to leave, Cindy buried her hands deeper in the satin-lined pockets of her heavy wool coat. It was too late to ring in the New Year with Thorne. Too late to believe that a relationship between them could work. Too late to demand her heart back!

Hunched against the piercing wind, her collar as close to her face as she could arrange it, Cindy turned and walked away. The tightness in her chest was nearly debilitating.

The sound of tires screeching to a halt and a car door slamming startled her.

"Cindy!"

She turned around sharply to discover Thorne frantically racing toward her.

Breathless, he caught her in his arms and held her to him. Roughly he pushed the hair from her face as though he needed to read her face and see for himself that she was safe and secure in his arms. "Oh, dear God, Cindy, I'm sorry, so sorry."

Every wild suspicion died the minute Thorne reached for her. He was so unbelievably warm and he held her as though he planned to do it a good long while. "You came," she murmured, laughing with pure relief. "You came." She wound her arms around his middle and tucked her head beneath his chin, savoring the warm, masculine feel of him. She noted there was something different about his usually distinctive masculine scent, as if it were mingled with some other fragrance.... But she was too deliriously happy at being in his arms to puzzle it out right now.

"You must be half-frozen," Thorne moaned, nuzzling her hair.

"Three-quarters," she jested. "But it was worth every second just to be with you now."

He kissed her then, his mouth cherishing hers, hungry yet gentle, demanding yet tender. Cindy absorbed his warmth, focusing on him like a tropical orchid turning toward the sun, seeking its nourishing rays as the source of all life.

Thorne lifted his head, cupped her chilled face with both hands and released a sigh that came from deep within him. He'd been overwrought, checking his watch every ten seconds, half crazy with fear that she'd walk out of his life and he'd never find her again. The traffic had been a nightmare, with the streets crammed with cars and people. His progress had been severely impeded until he'd decided he could arrive faster if he'd walked. He hadn't dreamed she'd still be there waiting, although he prayed she was. An hour she'd stood and waited in the freezing cold. He cursed Sheila and then himself.

"Let's get out of here," he said breathlessly. Looping his arm around her waist, he led her back to the taxi and helped her inside. He paused long enough to give the driver instructions to a drive to a nearby restaurant.

Once inside the cab, Cindy removed her shoes and started to rub some feeling back into her numb toes.

"Let me do that," Thorne insisted, placing her nylon-covered feet between his large hands and rubbing vigorously.

Cindy sighed, relaxed and leaned against the back of the cushioned seat.

"Any better?"

She nodded, content just to be with Thorne. "Where are we going?"

"Someplace where I can get some Irish coffee down you."

"I'm Italian," she said with a generous smile.

"Italian?" He eyed her curiously, surprised at her unexpected announcement. "But you're blond."

"There are plenty of us, trust me."

They arrived at the restaurant, but it wasn't one that Cindy recognized. Thorne gave her his hand to help her climb out of the taxi. He paid the driver and escorted her inside the lounge. They were given a table immediately, although the place was crowded. Cindy was convinced the large bill Thorne passed the maître d' had something to do with the waiting table.

Once they were seated, Thorne leaned against the back of the oak chair and ran a hand over his face. "I feel like I've been running a marathon," he said, expelling his breath.

"What happened?"

The waitress arrived and Thorne placed their order for drinks, glad for the interruption. He was going to mislead Cindy. It was only a lie of omission, but it still didn't sit right with him. He expected her to be honest with him, and it felt wrong to be less so with her. "I miscalculated the time and got caught in traffic. I didn't dare to hope you'd still be there; I don't know what I would have done if you'd left."

"I'd already decided to contact you in the morning."

He momentarily closed his eyes. "Thank God for that."

"You wanted to give us—the unprincely Thorne and the unadorned Cinderella—a chance, and I agreed, didn't I?"

"Yes."

His smile was capable of delaying an ice age, Cindy determined. He looked at her the way a starving man would survey a Thanksgiving feast. His gaze was tender and loving, warm and enticing. "We didn't ring in the New Year." His words revealed his regret.

"I know." She dropped her gaze because looking at him was much too intense, like staring into the sun for too long. She was becoming blind to the facts that surrounded their unusual relationship, ignoring the overwhelming potential for injury.

The waitress arrived with their drinks and Cindy sipped the liquor-laced coffee. It was hot, sweet and potent, burning a path down her throat and instantly spreading its warmth to her farthest extremities. The tingling sensation left her toes and fingers almost immediately.

"Next year we'll make it to Times Square?" Thorne suggested, his voice lifting slightly on the end of the statement, turning it into a question.

"Next year," she agreed, desperately wanting to believe they would be together twelve months from now. It was preferable not to look ahead with Thorne, to live for the moment, but she couldn't help herself.

"Are you hungry?" he asked next.

"Famished." She hadn't eaten anything since early afternoon, not wanting to spoil her appetite.

"Good. Do you want to order dinner now or would you rather have another cocktail?"

"Dinner," Cindy returned confidently. "But if you want another drink, don't let me stop you."

He picked up the menu and shook his head. "I've had a bottle of wine and a couple of cocktails before I caught up with you."

Cindy lifted the menu and mulled over the information he'd let slip. He'd lost track of the time, he'd claimed. That's easy enough to do when having a good time in the company of a beautiful woman. Her earlier suspicions resurrected themselves, bubbling to the surface of her mind like fizz in club soda—popping and hissing with doubts. Thorne had been with Sheila. He'd brought in the New Year with the other woman when he had asked to share the moment with her. He hadn't been with Cindy, but with Sheila, the woman whose picture sat prominently on his desk. Cindy was as convinced he'd been with the other woman as she was that the faint scent she'd noted on Thorne's jacket earlier was perfume. Sheila's perfume.

All the special excitement she experienced every time she was with Thorne whooshed out of her like air from a punctured balloon. She felt wounded. The commotion and noise from the restaurant that surrounded her seemed to fade into nothingness.

"Have you decided?" Thorne asked.

She stared at him blankly, not understanding what he was asking until she realized he was inquiring about her dinner selection. "No. What do you suggest?" It amazed her that she could speak coherently. There would be no next year for them—probably not even a next week. She'd be astonished if they made it through dinner.

You're overreacting, she told herself. *He had a drink with another woman. Big deal.* Thorne wasn't her exclusive property. But he'd obviously held Sheila, wrapped his arms around her... even kissed her. He must have, or the cloying scent of expensive perfume wouldn't be wafting from him.

Deliberately she set the menu aside and glared at him, not knowing what to do.

"Cindy?"

"Hum?" She made a conscious effort to look attentive.

"What's wrong? You don't look right."

"I'm fine," she lied. How could she be anything close to normal when the fragile walls of hope and expectation were crumbling at her feet? Her dreams had become ashes, burning hotly. Again she told herself that she was making too much of it. She had little to go on but conjecture, yet in her heart she knew. Thorne had left her standing in the miserable cold, alone, while he toasted the New Year with Sheila.

"If you'll excuse me a minute, I think I'd like to freshen up." Somehow she managed to keep her voice level, revealing none of the emotion that rocked her heart and her head.

"Of course." He stood when she did, but as she moved to turn away, his hand reached for her, stopping her. A frown marred his face. "There are tears in your eyes."

She hadn't realized she was crying. She rubbed the moisture from her face. "What would I have to cry about?" The words came out as if she were riding on a roller coaster, heaving in pitch, squeezing between the tightness that gripped her throat.

"You tell me."

Cindy reached for her coat and purse, the tears flowing in earnest now. The one drink had gone to her head on an empty stomach and she swayed slightly. "I suddenly figured everything out. I lost the feeling in my toes waiting for you."

Thorne blinked. She wasn't making the least bit of sense. "What do your toes have to do with the fact that you're crying?"

She jabbed a finger in his direction. "You... were... with... Sheila, weren't you?"

His chin jutted out with determination and fiery anger. He forced her to sit down and took the chair directly across from her. He wouldn't back down from the fierce anger in her gaze. She accused him of a multitude of crimes with one searing glare, and Thorne realized his mistake: he should have leveled with her earlier—he would have if he hadn't feared exactly this reaction. "Yes, I was with Sheila."

She leaned halfway across the small table, her eyes spitting fire. "For more than an hour I waited in the cold and wind, never once doubting you'd come. You're right, Thorne, you're no Prince Charming.''

''At the moment there isn't the faintest resemblance between you and Cinderella, either.''

She ignored that. ''If I had the least bit of magic left in me, I'd turn you into a frog.''

''I'd make you kiss me.'' Lord, he loved her. They were actually arguing, laying their feelings on the table the way a world-class poker player would turn over his cards.

''I don't think it would do any good,'' Cindy said hotly. ''Me kissing you, that is. You'd still be a frog.''

''That could be, but I sincerely doubt it.''

Cindy bit into her bottom lip. Thorne seemed to think this witty exchange was fun while she was devastated. He was so casual about it, and that hurt.

Thorne immediately sensed the change in Cindy. ''I didn't want to be with Sheila,'' he said, his eyes dark and serious. ''I begrudged every minute that I wasn't with you.''

Cindy didn't know what to believe anymore.

''Then why...''

''I was trapped,'' he said, and although his voice revealed his pride, his eyes pleaded with her for understanding. ''I would have given anything to welcome in the New Year with you. God willing, I will next year.''

Hours later, when she crawled into bed, she wasn't any more confident than she had been in the restaurant. They'd both ordered lobster and talked for hours, their earlier dispute quickly shelved because their time together was too precious to waste arguing. It astonished Cindy the way they could talk. They liked the same things, shared the same interests, bounced ideas off each other and lingered so long over coffee that the waitress grew restless. Only then did Cindy and Thorne notice that they were the only couple left in the restaurant.

"When can I see you again?" he asked.

"Soon," she promised, buttoning her coat. "I'll contact you."

He hadn't liked that, Cindy could tell by the hard set of his mouth. Before they parted, he made her promise that she'd get in touch with him. She would.

Now, as early-morning shadows danced across the walls, Cindy lay in her bed undecided. Because she'd given Thorne her word, she would meet him, but this had to be the end of it. Oh, heavens, how often had she said that? Too often. And each time, walking away from him had grown more difficult. He was like an addictive drug, trapping her more with each contact, filling her with longing for him. He was so wonderfully good for her and so disastrously bad for her. She didn't know what she was going to do anymore. Thorne was in her blood.

Thorne stood on the dock as large sea gulls circled overhead. The Staten Island ferry, filled with crowds of tourists who'd taken the twenty-five-cent ride for a closer view of the Statue of Liberty, was slowly advancing toward the long pier.

Cindy had said she'd meet him here. She hadn't shown up yet, but it was still too early to be concerned. It had been a week since he'd last seen her. His fault, not hers. He'd been out of town on business and had returned home to find a note taped to his apartment door. She'd set the time and the place for this meeting. How she'd known he would be free this afternoon was beyond him. Where and how she got her information no longer concerned him. Seeing and being with her were of primary importance. Nothing else mattered.

He had to find a way to assure her that she was the most important person in his life. The incident with Sheila had been left unsettled between them. Thorne could see from Cindy's taut features that she wanted to believe that whatever he shared with Sheila was over. But she had her doubts, and he couldn't blame her.

Briefly he thought about the large diamond he kept in the safe at the office. He wanted it on her finger and her promise to be his wife, but he knew better than to ask her, although the question burned in him like a smoldering fire. The timing had to be right. It wasn't yet. When she completely trusted him, when she opened up to him and told him everything, then he could offer her his life.

For now, all he could do was love her, dispel the doubts one at a time. Today he'd come up with a way of doing that.

"Hi." Cindy joined him on the dock. Her hands were buried deep inside her pockets as she stood, looking into the wind.

Slow, grateful relief poured over Thorne like thick honey. She'd come; he could relax and smile again.

"Hi, yourself," he responded with a smile, resisting the urge to take her in his arms.

"How was Kansas City?"

He smiled, because she'd amazed him again. She'd known where he'd been and for how long. "Dull. I was in a rush to get back to you. Did you miss me?"

Cindy nodded, although she'd rather not admit as much. The week they'd spent apart had seemed a lifetime. For seven days she'd told herself she'd better get used to living without him being the focal point of her existence. "School started up again, I've been busy."

"But you still thought about me?"

Every minute of every day. "Yes," she answered starkly.

The ferry docked and they stood and watched silently as the passengers disembarked.

"I haven't been to the Statue of Liberty since it's been refurbished, have you?" Thorne asked, watching her. It was obvious something was troubling her. Cindy wasn't this quiet this long, without something weighing on her mind.

"No." The wind swirled her hair around her face and she lifted a strand of hair from her cheek.

Thorne studied her. She looked so troubled, so uncertain that he gently pulled her into his embrace, holding her close.

She sighed and leaned against him, relishing his touch after seven tedious days of being without him. She'd never be the same after Thorne. She would go on with her life because there was no option to do anything else. But she'd never be the same.

"Are you ready to talk?" he asked softly, raising her chin so she would meet his gaze.

At one time she had been, but not anymore. It seemed they took one step forward, then quickly retreated two. Just when she was beginning to feel secure and right about loving him he'd left her waiting while he was with Sheila. Although he'd repeatedly claimed the other woman meant nothing to him, he continued to keep her picture on prominent display on his desk. And recently, quite by accident, she discovered the receipt from Tiffany's for a diamond ring. If she'd been insecure about her position in Thorne's life before, now she was paranoid.

"Cindy?" he prompted.

Sadly she shook her head, then brightened. "Shall we walk along the water to get in line for the Statue of Liberty ferry?"

"No."

"You don't want to go?"

"I have a surprise for you."

"A surprise?" Her heart rocketed to her throat.

He reached for her hand. "We're going someplace special today."

"Where?"

"That's the surprise." He smiled down on her and reached for her hand.

Again Cindy was convinced dinosaurs would still be roaming the world if Thorne's smile had been around to halt the flowing ice.

"My car's parked down the street."

"Your car?"

"We can't reach . . . this place by subway."

Despite her reservations, Cindy laughed. "I'm not sure I like surprises."

"This one you will." His fingers tightened around hers. "I promise." Cindy would know for certain her position in his life after today.

"Are you sure this is . . . someplace I want to go?"

"Now that may be in question, but you've already agreed."

"I did? When?"

Thorne kissed the top of her nose. "The night we met."

Cindy shuffled through her memories and came back blank. "I don't recall agreeing to anything."

Thorne pretended shock, then shook his head in mock despair. "How quickly they forget."

"Thorne!" He led her up the street.

"This isn't anyplace fancy is it?" She wore crisp blue jeans, a pink turtleneck sweater and loafers with hot pink socks.

"You're perfect no matter what you wear."

"I suppose this is some fancy restaurant where everyone will be in a tux."

"No restaurant."

"But we are eating?" She certainly hoped they would be. As usual, she was starving. Why, oh, why did it always happen this way? She'd be so uneasy, so certain nothing would ever work between them, and ten minutes after being with Thorne, she would gladly hand over her soul. The thought of being separated from him was unthinkable. She was crazy in love with this man.

"Are you worried about your stomach again?"

"Don't worry, it's something lobster will cure," she joked and was rewarded with a smile.

Cindy would have bet anything Thorne drove a Mercedes in a subdued shade of gray or steely blue. She was wrong—his car was a Corvette, bright red and so unlike him that she stood with her hands on her hips and shook her head.

"I bought it on impulse," he said a bit sheepishly, holding open the passenger door for her.

She climbed inside, amazed at how close to the ground they were. When she had trouble with the seat belt, Thorne leaned over and snapped it into place, teasing her unmercifully about her lack of mechanical ability, then kissing her soundly when she blushed.

Once they were on the Jersey turnpike, Cindy grew all the more curious. "Just how many days will we be traveling?"

"Forty-five minutes," he answered.

"That long, huh? Aren't you going to give me any clues?"

Thorne resolutely shook his head. "Not anything more than I've already told you."

He was in such a good mood that it was impossible to be serious. Soon they were both laughing, and Cindy didn't notice when he exited from the freeway. He drove confidently through a neighborhood of luxurious homes.

"This must be quite some place."

"Oh, it is," he promised.

When he turned into a long circular driveway that curved around a huge water fountain, Cindy's curiosity was all the more sharp. She'd never seen a more opulent home. Two floors with huge white pillars dominated the front. It looked like something out of *Architectural Digest*.

"Wow." She couldn't find any other word to describe it.

The front door opened and a lovely gray-haired woman stepped out to greet Thorne. The older woman's gaze rested on Cindy, and although she revealed little emotion, Cindy had the impression the woman disapproved of her.

Thorne climbed out of the car and stepped around and kissed the woman on the cheek.

A rock settled in the pit of Cindy's stomach as Thorne opened her door and offered his hand to help her out.

"Cindy," he said, "I'd like you to meet my mother."

Chapter Nine

Cindy's introduction to Thorne's parents was strained at best. She was enraged that he would bring her to his family home without a word to prepare her. Even worse, he'd informed her that what she was wearing was perfectly fine. He couldn't have been more wrong. Jeans and a turtleneck sweater weren't the least bit acceptable if Gwendolyn Prince's look told Cindy anything. Cindy would have been more comfortable being unexpectedly granted an audience with the Pope.

Seated beside Thorne in the extravagant living room, Cindy rotated the stem of a crystal wineglass between her palms. Although Thorne's mother was subtle about it, Cindy could feel the other woman studying her. His father's gray eyes sparkled with undisguised delight. He, at least, seemed to be enjoying this farce.

"Where was it you said you met?" the elder Thorne asked.

"The company Christmas party."

Cindy let Thorne answer for her. Her mouth felt dry, and she wasn't sure her tongue would cooperate if she did try to speak.

"So you're employed by Oakes-Jenning?"

This time the question was shot directly at Cindy.

"Dad," Thorne interrupted smoothly. "I think I'll let you get me a refill." He held out his glass to his father, who stood and poured the clear wine.

The elder Prince silently offered Cindy a refill, but she refused with a short shake of her head. If there was ever a time she needed to keep her wits, it was now. Forget the audience with the Pope, she would have been more comfortable in a torture chamber. The minute she was alone with Thorne, she'd let him know what she thought of his "surprise."

"I don't believe I caught your last name?" His mother asked, eyeing Cindy.

"Territo. Cindy Territo." Her voice came out sounding like she was on her deathbed. Cindy felt as if she were.

"That sounds ethnic," Thorne's mother commented, not unkindly.

"It's . . ." Cindy began.

"Italian," Thorne finished.

"I see." His mother obviously didn't.

Cindy watched as the older woman downed the remainder of her wine. She appeared as uneasy as Cindy.

"Thorne tells me you're a student?" His father continued the inquisition.

"Yes, I'm studying computer programming."

This, too, was news to Thorne. He knew Cindy was uncomfortable answering all these questions. He'd asked his parents to make her feel welcome, but he should have known better than to suggest they not intimidate her with rounds of inquiries. His father was too cagey to let the opportunity pass. Thorne reached for Cindy's hand and was astonished to discover that her fingers were as cold as ice.

"I'm sure Cindy is just as curious about us," Thorne said, squeezing her hand reassuringly. "Why don't we let her ask what she'd like to know about us?"

"I . . . know everything I need to," she murmured with a feeble smile. The instant the words were out, Cindy wanted to grab them back, realizing she'd said the wrong thing. She'd made it sound as if all she cared about was Thorne's money. Nothing could be less true. She would have fallen in love with Thorne had he sold pencils on a street corner. Now, in addition to being ill at ease, she was acutely embarrassed.

Dinner did little to help. They sat at a long table with a crystal chandelier she suspected was worth more than her uncle's limousine. Thorne sat across from her, making her feel all the more alone. His parents dominated both ends of the long table.

A large glass of ice rested in front of Cindy, and her mouth was so uncomfortably dry that she reached for it, disappointed to find so little water inside. Thorne's mother gave her a pathetic glance and instantly Cindy realized that she'd committed some terrible faux pas. Her mortification reached a peak when the maid delivered a shrimp cocktail, placing the appetizer inside the glass of ice. Only then did Cindy realize the glass wasn't meant for water. Cindy died a little at that moment. If there had been a hole to hide in, she would have sought it, burying herself with blanket after blanket of humiliation. She dared not look at Thorne, certain he would find the entire incident amusing.

"What does your father do?" Gwendolyn asked, between bites of succulent shrimp.

Briefly Cindy closed her eyes to gather her composure. She'd already disgraced Thorne with her lack of finesse once, she'd be damned before she did so again. "I'm afraid I don't know...he deserted my mother and me shortly after I was born."

"Oh, my dear, how terrible for your mother."

"She's gone as well, isn't she?" Thorne asked almost absently, studying Cindy. His loving gaze caressed her, his brow distorted with concern.

"She died when I was five."

"Who raised you?" It was the elder Thorne who questioned her now. From the looks they were giving her, one would have thought she'd been beaten daily and survived on dry bread crumbs tossed under the table.

"My aunt and uncle were kind enough to raise me." Thorne's parents exchanged sympathetic glances. "Believe me," Cindy hurried to add. "There's no need to feel sorry for me. They loved me as they would their own daughter. We're a close-knit family with lots of cousins and assorted relatives." Her aunt and uncle, however, wouldn't dream of interrogating Thorne the way his parents were questioning her.... Then again maybe they would. Cindy felt slightly better musing about how her Uncle Sal would react to meeting Thorne. The first hint of amusement touched the edges of her mouth. She raised her gaze to meet Thorne's and they shared a brief smile.

Dinner couldn't be over soon enough for Cindy. She ate only enough to assure that no one would comment. The prime rib rested like a lead weight in the pit of her stomach. Dessert, a frothy concoction of lime and whipped cream, was a cool respite, and she managed to consume a large portion of that.

"While the women have their coffee, let me show you my new nine iron." The elder Prince addressed his son.

Thorne's gaze met Cindy's. She nodded, assuring him that she'd be fine left alone with his mother. She was confident that Gwendolyn Prince had arranged this time so the two women could speak frankly, and Cindy was prepared to do exactly that.

The men left the table.

Cindy took a sip of her coffee and braced herself. She noted that Thorne's mother's hand shook slightly and she was reassured to realize that the old woman was equally nervous.

Neither spoke for a long moment.

"Mrs. Prince—"

"Cindy—"

They both began at the same instant and laughed, flustered and uneasy.

"You first, dear," Gwendolyn said.

Cindy straightened the linen napkin on her lap. "I wanted to apologize for drinking out of the wrong glass..." She paused, drew in a deep, steadying breath, deciding to do away with small talk and get to the point. "I believe I know what you want to say, and I couldn't agree with you more. You're absolutely right about me. It's perfectly obvious that Thorne and I are terribly ill suited."

If the older woman's hand had trembled before, now it positively shook. "Why, Cindy, what makes you suggest such a thing?"

"You mean other than my drinking from the shrimp boat?"

The first indication that Thorne's mother was capable of a smile showed on the older woman's ageless face. "My dear girl, shall I tell you about the time I drank too much wine and told Thorndike's mother that she was a cantankerous old biddy?"

Cindy raised the napkin to her mouth to disguise her laugh. "You honestly said that?"

"And he proposed the next day. He told me he needed a wife who would stand up to his mother. I'd been crazy about him for years, you see, and I didn't think he knew I was alive. We'd been dating off and on for months—mostly on—and our relationship seemed to be moving sideways. That Sunday dinner with his family was the turning point in our courtship."

"And you've enjoyed a happy marriage." Cindy made it a statement, confident that the Prince marriage had been a good one.

"Over forty years now."

Silence followed.

"I want you to know that little of what Thorndike and I say will influence our son. He's always been his own man, and he hasn't brought you here for our approval."

Cindy nodded, agreeing that Thorne wouldn't be intimidated by his family's reservations regarding her. "You don't need to say anything more, I understand."

"But I feel confident that you don't," Gwendolyn said hurriedly. "It's just that Thorne and Sheila were such an item that both Thorndike and I assumed...well, we naturally thought that he and Sheila...oh dear, I do seem to be making a mess of this."

"It would only seem natural that after all those months they would marry."

"And then out of the blue, Thorne mentioned meeting you." Gwendolyn looked flustered and reached for her coffee.

Cindy dropped her gaze. The Christmas Ball and her little charade did seem to have tossed a fly in the ointment.

"Thorne thinks highly of you."

"You and your husband must be special people to have raised a son as wonderful as Thorne." Cindy meant that sincerely. "He's touched my life in ways I'll always remember."

"I do believe you mean that."

"I do, but I realized early on that I'm not the woman for him. He needs a different type." Although she would have given anything in this world to be wrong, she knew she wasn't.

Gwendolyn's cup made a clanging sound when she set it in the saucer. "I don't suppose you've told Thorne that."

"Not yet."

"He won't give up on you easily."

Cindy agreed, remembering the detective. "He can be as stubborn as an ornery mule sometimes."

Gwendolyn laughed outright. "He's quite a bit like his father."

"I'm doing a poor job of expressing myself," Cindy said and her voice revealed her pain. "I want to reassure you that I won't upset you or your family by complicating Thorne's life."

"Oh dear," Gwendolyn looked stunned. "Now that I've met you, I was rather hoping you would."

The words were a soothing balm to Cindy. "Thank you."

"Oh, my," Gwendolyn touched her face with her fingertips. "I do wonder if I'm making an idiot of myself again. Thorndike swears I should never drink wine."

"He married you because of it," Cindy reminded the older woman, and they shared a smile.

"Thorne would never forgive me if I offended you."

"You haven't."

The men joined them a minute later and Thorne's searching gaze sought out Cindy's. She reassured him with a smile that everything had gone well between her and his mother and she saw him relax visibly. He'd been worried for nothing. She hadn't been raised in a large family without learning how to hold her own.

Thorne gave his parents a weak excuse and they left shortly afterward. Instead of heading toward the freeway, Thorne drove into a church parking lot and turned off the engine.

"My father was impressed with you."

"I can't imagine why," Cindy returned honestly.

He ignored that. "What did my mother have to say?"

"What I expected."

"Which was?" he probed.

Cindy shook her head. "We came to an understanding."

"Good or bad?"

"Good. I like her, Thorne, she's direct and honest."

He rubbed his hand along the back of her neck. "So are you, love," he said softly and directed her mouth to his, kissing her hungrily.

"So, Cindy Territo, it wasn't such a hard thing to reveal your name, was it?" He brushed his mouth over hers, his mouth nipping at her bottom lip with tiny, biting kisses.

"No." Nothing was difficult when she was in his arms. Since the Christmas Ball, she'd allowed his velvet touch to confuse the issue. She'd be so certain of what she had to do, and then he'd kiss her and she'd fall at his feet. It wasn't fair for him to have such an overwhelming effect on her. She wasn't weak-willed, nor was her character lacking. She hadn't once suspected that love would do this to a person.

Her aunt was knitting in front of the television set when Cindy let herself into the apartment. Cindy glanced at her aunt, said nothing and moved into the kitchen. Theresa put down the yarn and needles and followed her niece.

"So how was the Statue of Liberty?"

"We didn't go there." Her voice was strained with emotion.

"Oh." Her aunt opened the oven door and basted the turkey roasting inside. "So where'd you go?"

"Thorne took me to meet his family."

Surprised, Theresa let the oven door close with a bang. "His family? You must mean a great deal to him. So how did the introductions go?"

Cindy took a pitcher of orange juice from the refrigerator and poured herself a glass, but not because she was thirsty. She was merely looking for something, anything, to occupy her hands and her mind. "I met his mother and father and . . . nothing."

"'Nothing,' you say?"

Her aunt knew her too well for Cindy to try to fool the older woman. She set the glass of juice on the kitchen table and slumped into the chair, burying her face in her hands. A sob escaped and Cindy ruthlessly bit down on her bottom lip, hoping to squelch the flood of pent-up tears that demanded release.

Theresa placed her hand on Cindy's shoulder and patted gently. "Love hurts, doesn't it, honey?"

"I've been fooling myself . . . it's just not going to work. I made such an idiot of myself . . . and everyone was so nice. Thorne pretended not to notice, and his mother assured me she'd done silly things in her life, and his father just looked at me like I was an alien from outer space. I could have died."

"I'm sure that whatever you did wasn't as bad as you think."

"It was worse!" she cried.

"Right now you think it is," Theresa stated calmly. "Give it a year or so and you'll look back and laugh at yourself."

Cindy couldn't visualize laughing about anything at the moment. She was hurting too much. She raised her head, sniffled and wiped the moisture from her face with the back of her hand.

"I've decided. I'm not going to see him again," Cindy said with iron determination, promising herself as well as informing her family of her resolution. "It isn't going to work, and confusing the issues with love won't change a thing."

"Did you tell Thorne that?"

Miserably, Cindy shook her head. "I didn't want to invite an argument." She couldn't bear to spend their last minutes together debating her decision. Thorne had taken her to meet his family to prove how easily she'd fit in, and the opposite had proven true. She'd enjoyed his parents. She couldn't imagine not liking the two people most influential in Thorne's upbringing. They were decent folks and his mother was a kick, but Cindy had known the minute she'd walked inside their home that the chasm that divided their life-styles was far too wide ever to bridge.

She glanced around the Territo family kitchen at the heavy mahogany dining-room table with plain wooden chairs that had once belonged to her grandmother. There were no plush Persian carpets or Oriental rugs beneath their table, only worn hardwood floors. Their furniture was simple, as were their lives. Comparing the two families would be like trying to mix spaghetti sauce with lobster.

Before they parted, Thorne had asked to meet her again. Distraught and too weak to argue with him, Cindy had agreed. Now she was sorry.

"The man's in love with you," Theresa said simply.

"But encouraging him will only hurt him more."

Theresa sadly shook her head. "Are you saying you don't love him?"

"Yes," Cindy cried, then bit her lower lip at the searing look her aunt gave her. "I love him," she admitted finally, "but that doesn't make everything right. Some things in life were meant to be; other relationships can never be right."

Her aunt gave her a troubled look. "You're old enough to know what you want. I'm not going to stand here and argue with you. Anything I say is unlikely to change your mind, since it's obvious you've thought about this a great deal. But I want you to know that you're a marvelous girl and a man like Thorndike Prince wouldn't fall in love with you if you weren't."

Cindy's head bobbed up and down. For now he may have convinced himself that he loved her, but later, after he knew her better, he'd regret his love. Because of the unusual circumstances of their relationship he looked upon her as a challenge. It hurt, but she'd made her decision, and although it was the most difficult thing she'd ever done in her life, she was determined to stick by it.

"Yes." Thorne flipped the intercom switch, his eyes remaining on the report he was studying. Interruptions were part of his day and he'd grown accustomed to doing several things at once when necessary.

Mrs. Hillard paused and cleared her throat. "Your mother is here."

Thorne released the button and groaned inwardly. He may be able to have Mrs. Hillard fend off unexpected and unwanted visits from Sheila, but his mother wouldn't easily be put off by his secretary's excuses. He pressed the button. "Go ahead and send her in."

"Thorne." His mother sauntered into the office, her face a cheerful facade.

He stood and kissed her on the cheek, already guessing that she was concerned about something. "To what do I owe this unexpected pleasure?" She wore her full-length fur coat, and absently Thorne thought about how Cindy would look in fox. No, he decided absently, with her blond hair, he'd buy her mink. He'd give it to her as an engagement present when they set their wedding date. He was anxious to give her all the things she deserved. She'd given him so much in such a little time that it would take a lifetime to repay her.

"I was in town and thought I'd let you take me to lunch."

His mother had obviously taught Sheila the same trick. "What about Dad?"

"He's tied up in a meeting."

"Ah." Understanding came.

"Besides, I wanted to talk to you."

Unexpectedly Thorne bristled, automatically suspicious of her intentions. His mother wanted to discuss Cindy. He knew it as clearly as if she'd stormed into his office and demanded they talk about the Italian woman he'd brought to their family home. He sighed, sensing an argument.

"What's the name of that nice little restaurant you like so well?" his mother asked, rearranging the small items on top of his desk, irritating him further.

"Tastings."

"Right. I made reservations at the Russian Tea Room."

Thorne managed to nod. It didn't matter where they ate or what they ate, as long as the air was clear when they'd finished.

Half an hour later, Thorne studied his mother as they sat in a plush booth in the Russian Tea Room. Methodically she removed her white gloves one finger at a time. He knew her well enough to realize she was stalling.

"You wanted to say something, Mother?" He had no desire to delay the confrontation. If she disapproved of Cindy, he'd prefer to have it in the open and over with quickly. Not that anything she said would alter his feelings toward the woman he loved. He'd prefer it if his family approved, but he wouldn't let them stand in his way.

"Sheila phoned me this morning and I'm afraid I may have done something you'd rather I hadn't." She tossed him an apologetic glance and reached for the menu, hiding behind it.

Thorne's fingers tightened around the water glass. "Perhaps it would be best if you started from the beginning."

"The beginning... Well, yes, I do suppose I should." She set the menu aside. "I think you already know that I've had my reservations about Cindy."

"Listen, Mother, let me assure you that your feelings about Cindy mean little to me. I love her and, God willing, I plan to marry her and..."

"Please, allow me to finish." She seared him with a look she hadn't used since his youth. Her words were sharp and clipped. "As it happens, I find your Cindy to be a delight."

"You do?"

"Don't be a ninny! She's marvelous; now quit acting so surprised." She shook her head lightly. "I thought at first that she might be too shy and retiring for you, which put me in a terrible position, since I sincerely doubted you'd care one way or the other what I thought of her. But as it happens, I like her. That girl's got pluck."

"Pluck?"

"Right. I'm pleased to hear you have the good sense to want to marry her."

Thorne was so astonished he nearly slid out of the booth and onto the floor. "I have every intention of making her my wife as soon as possible. She may put up a fight, but I'm not taking no for an answer."

His mother made an art of straightening the silverware, aligning each piece just so. "Well, dear, there may be a small problem."

"Yes?"

"Sheila seems quite broken up with the news that I happen to give my wholehearted approval of Cindy. Mentioning that you'd brought her by to meet your father and me may not have been my finest hour. I had no idea Sheila would react so negatively. I fear the girl may try to create problems for you."

"Let her." Thorne dealt with sensitive situations every day. He could handle Sheila. He'd calm her and end their relationship on a friendly note. "Don't worry, Mother, Sheila has been well aware of my feelings for Cindy for quite some time."

"She did seem to think you'd change your mind."

Thorne's mouth thinned with impatience. "She knows better."

"I'm worried about her, Thorne. I want you to talk to her."

Thorne's fingers smoothed the fork tines. "Okay. I'm not sure it will help. I regret any emotional trauma I may have caused her, but I'm not going to do anything more than talk to her."

"Do it soon."

Thorne agreed, elated with the information of his family's acceptance of Cindy. With clarity he recalled the look on her face when he'd last left her. She'd clung to him and kissed him with such fervor that it had been difficult to leave her. He thought about Cindy as his wife and the years that stretched before him like a golden pathway—a lifetime filled with happiness and love. Even though he'd considered marrying Sheila at one point, he'd never thought about their future the way he did with Cindy, plotting their happiness.

"I'm seeing her tomorrow."

"Sheila?" his mother inquired.

Irritated, he shook his head. "No, Cindy."

"But you will talk to Sheila; I'm afraid she may do something silly."

"I'll speak to her," Thorne promised, determined to put an end to his relationship with the other woman.

Thorne stared at the wall clock in the lobby of the American Museum of Natural History. Cindy was half an hour late. It wasn't like her not to be punctual and he was mildly surprised. He had every minute of their evening planned. Dinner. Drinks. Dancing. Then they'd take a walk in Central Park and he'd bring out the diamond. The Tiffany ring burned a hole in is pocket. Tonight was it. He'd waited thirty-three years to find Cindy and he wasn't ever going to let her go.

All day he'd rehearsed what he intended to say. First he'd tell her how knowing her had changed his life. It wasn't only singing in the shower and noticing the birds and blooming flowers, either. Before she'd sashayed into his life, he'd fallen into a deep-grooved rut. His work had become meaningless, merely occupying his time. He'd lost his direction.

But her laughter and her smile had lifted him to the heavens, given him hope. He'd tell her that he'd never thought he'd experience the love he did for her. It had caught him unawares.

Naturally she'd be surprised by the suddenness of this proposal. She might even insist on an extended engagement. Of course, he hoped she'd agree immediately so they could set the date and begin to make the necessary arrangements for their wedding—a church wedding. He didn't want any rushed affair; when he made his vows to Cindy he wanted them spoken before God, not some fly-by-night justice of the peace. He intended their vows to last a lifetime.

Growing impatient, Thorne pulled the newspaper from his briefcase. Maybe if he read the snail-pace minutes would go by faster. He scanned the business news and reached for the front page when the society section slipped to the floor.

Thorne retrieved it and was surprised to find Sheila's face smiling benignly back at him. Interested, he turned the page right side up and read the headlines. SHEILA MATHEWSON ANNOUNCES PLANS TO MARRY THORNDIKE PRINCE.

Thorne roared to his feet like a lion preparing to attack. The paper in his hand was crumpled into a wadded mass. So this was what his mother had come to prepare him for.... And worse, this was the reason Cindy hadn't arrived.

Chapter Ten

The minute Cindy walked into the apartment, her Aunt Theresa and Uncle Sal abruptly cut off their conversation. Cindy paused and studied their flushed faces; it wasn't difficult to ascertain that the two had been in the midst of a rousing argument. The instant Cindy arrived, they both seemed to find things to occupy their hands. Her aunt opened the refrigerator and brought out a head of lettuce and her uncle reached for a deck of cards, shuffling them again and again, his gaze centered on his hands.

"I'll be in my room," Cindy said, granting them privacy. She was sorry they were arguing, and although it was uncommon, she knew from experience it was best to let them resolve their differences without interference from her.

Sitting on the edge of her bed, Cindy eyed the clock. Thorne would be heading for the museum by now, anticipating their meeting. Only she wouldn't be there. She'd let him think she'd agreed to this date, but she hadn't confirmed anything.

Coward! her mind accused her harshly. But she had no option, Cindy argued back. Every time she was with Thorne, her objections melted like snow under a tropical sun. Her head was so boggled, so confused, she didn't know what she wanted anymore. Oh, she loved Thorne, she was convinced of that. But he was so easy to love. It would be far more difficult *not* to care for him.

Shaking her head vigorously, Cindy decided she couldn't leave Thorne waiting. That was childish and silly. It simply wasn't in her to let him waste his time worrying about her. She'd go to him and do her utmost to explain. All she wanted was some time apart. Some space to test their feelings. Everything had happened so quickly between them that it would be wrong to act impulsively now. True love can wait. A month was the amount of time she was going to suggest. That didn't seem so long. Thorne would have to promise not to see her until Valentine's Day. If he truly cared for her, he'd agree to that.

Once she'd made her decision—the third one in as many days—she acted purposefully. She had her scarf wrapped around her neck by the time she entered the kitchen. She paused to button her coat.

Her uncle took one look at her and asked, "Where are you headed?"

Sal so rarely questioned her about anything that his brusque inquiry now took her by surprise. "I'm...the museum."

"You're not meeting that Prince fellow, are you?"

Her aunt pinched her lips together tightly and slammed the kitchen drawer closed, obviously disapproving of Sal's interrogation.

Cindy's gaze flew from Theresa back to her uncle. "I had...yes, I planned to meet Thorne there."

"No."

"No? I don't understand."

"I said I don't want you to have anything to do with that rich, spoiled kid."

"But Uncle Sal—"

"The discussion is closed." Sal's hand slammed against the tabletop, upsetting the saltshaker.

Stunned, Cindy gasped and took a step backward. "I'm twenty-two years old. It's a little late to be telling me I can't meet someone."

"You are never to see that man again. Is that understood?"

"Cindy is old enough to make up her own mind," Theresa inserted calmly, her back to her husband.

"You keep out of this, woman."

"So the big Italian stallion thinks he can speak with all the authority of a supreme court judge," Theresa taunted, her face growing redder by the second. "And I say Cindy can meet her Prince anytime she wishes."

"And I say she can't!" Sal blared, turning around to face his wife.

"Uncle Sal, Aunt Theresa, please..."

"He's not good enough for you," Sal said, calmer this time, his eyes wide with appeal. "Not near good enough for our Cindy."

"Oh, Uncle Sal—"

"Cindy..."

The compassion in her aunt's eyes were so strong that Cindy forgot what she wanted to say.

The room went still, too quiet. Her uncle's gaze fell to the floor and the thick, dark lashes of Theresa's eyes glistened with moisture.

"Something happened." Cindy knew it as well as if they were shouting it at her. "It's Thorne, isn't jit?"

Her Aunt Theresa nodded, her troubled gaze avoiding Cindy's.

"Is he hurt?" Alarm filled her, bordering on panic. "Oh, you must tell me if he's injured. I couldn't bear it if he—"

"The man's a no-good bum. You're best rid of him."

It was all so terribly confusing. Everyone seemed to be speaking in riddles. Her gaze drifted from her uncle back to her aunt, pleading with them both to tell her and put an end to this nightmare of fear.

"I think we'd better tell her," Theresa said softly.

"No," Sal raged.

"Tell me what?"

"It's in the paper," Theresa explained gently.

"I said she doesn't need to know," Sal shouted, taking the evening paper and stuffing it in the garbage.

"Uncle Sal!" Cindy pleaded. "What is it?"

Theresa crossed the room and reached for Cindy's hand. The last time Cindy could remember seeing her aunt look at her in exactly that way had been when she was a child and Theresa had come to tell the five-year-old that her mother had gone to live in Heaven.

"What is it?" Cindy asked, her voice so low and weak that it wobbled between two octaves. "He's not dead. Oh, dear God, don't tell me he's dead."

"No, love." Her aunt said softly.

Some of the terrible tension left Cindy's frozen limbs.

Theresa closed her eyes briefly and glanced over her shoulder to her husband. "She'll find out sooner or later. It's better she hear it from us."

It seemed for a moment that Sal was going to argue. His chest swelled as though to heartily disagree, then quickly deflated with defeat. He looked so unlike his robust, outgoing self that Cindy couldn't imagine what was troubling him so.

"Sal read the announcement in the paper and brought it to me."

"The announcement?" Cindy asked.

"Thorne's marrying—"

"—some high-society dame," Sal concluded sharply. Regret shouted from every part of him as though he would have done anything to have spared Cindy this.

"But I don't understand," Cindy murmured, uncertain what she was hearing.

"It was listed in the society page."

"Sheila?"

Her aunt nodded.

Cindy sank into a kitchen chair, her legs unable to support her. "I'm sure there's some mistake, I . . . he took me to meet his family."

"He was using you," Sal murmured, coming to stand behind her. Gently his hands patted her shoulders as he'd done when she was a little girl, giving solace. "He was probably using his family to give you the impression he was serious so he could get you into his bed.''

''No,'' Cindy cried. ''No, it was never like that. Thorne didn't even suggest . . . not once.''

''Then thank God for that, that was where he was leading. He's a smart devil, I'll say that for him.''

Theresa claimed the chair next to Cindy and reached for her numb fingers, rubbing them. ''I refused to believe it myself until Sal showed me the article. But there it was, bold as can be. It's true, Cindy.''

Cindy nodded, accepting what her family was telling her as truth. No tears burned for release. No hysterical sob brewed deep within her. She felt nothing. No pain. No sense of betrayal. No anger. Nothing.

''Are you going to be all right?'' Theresa asked softly.

''I'll be fine. Don't worry. It was inevitable, you know. I think I accepted it from the beginning. Something deep inside me always realized he could never be mine.''

''But . . . oh, Cindy, I can hardly believe it myself.''

Cindy stood and hugged her aunt close. ''You fell for the magic,'' she whispered gently. ''So did I for a time. But you see, I'm not really Cinderella and Thorne isn't really a prince. It had to end sometime.''

''But I hurt so much for you!'' Theresa sobbed.

''Don't. I'm not nearly as upset as you think,'' Cindy murmured.

Theresa straightened and wiped her face free of tears.

''I'm going to study for a while.'' She was fighting off the terrible numbness, knowing she had to do something. Anything. Otherwise she'd go crazy.

Sal slipped an arm around his wife and Theresa pressed her head to his shoulder. "Okay," Sal told his niece softly. "You hit those books and you'll feel better."

Cindy walked back to her room and closed the door. It seemed so dingy inside. Dingy and gray. She didn't feel like studying, but she forced herself to sit on the mattress and open her textbook. The words blurred, swimming in and out of her focus, and Cindy was shocked to realize she was crying.

"I want a retraction and I want it printed in today's paper," Thorne raged at the society-page editor. The poor woman was red with indignation, but Thorne was beyond caring.

"I've already explained that we won't be able to do that until tomorrow's paper," the woman said patiently for the sixth time.

"But that could be too late."

"I apologize for any inconvenience this may have caused you, Mr. Prince, but we received Ms. Mathewson's announcement through the normal channels. I can assure you this kind of thing is most unusual."

"And you printed the wedding announcement without checking with the proposed groom?"

The woman sat at her desk, holding the pencil at each end with a grip so hard it threatened to snap it. "Let me assure you, Mr. Prince, that in all my years in the newspaper business, this is the first bogus wedding announcement that has ever crossed my desk. In the past there's never been any need to verify the event with the proposed groom—or bride for that matter."

"Then maybe you should start."

"Perhaps," she returned stiffly. "Now, if you'll excuse me, I've got work to do."

"You haven't heard the end of this," Thorne said heatedly.

"I don't doubt it," the editor returned with spirit.

Thorne did an abrupt about-face and left the newspaper office, unconcerned with the amount of attention his argument had caused.

On the street, he caught the first taxi he could flag down and headed back to the office. As it was, he was working on a tight schedule. He'd already attended an important meeting early that morning—one he'd tried to postpone and couldn't. The minute he was free, he'd had Mrs. Hillard contact Mike Williams, and he'd paced restlessly until he'd learned that Mike was out of town on a case and not expected back for another week.

The detective could well be his only chance of finding Cindy. Mike had gotten close to her once, but after Cindy had shown up outside his office building, Thorne had done as she requested and asked Mike to halt his investigation. After all, he'd gotten what he'd wanted—Cindy was back. Now he wished he'd pursued it further. She'd left him and he had no more chance of finding her now than when she'd left him the night of the Christmas Ball.

A feeling of desperation swamped Thorne. When Cindy hadn't shown at the museum, Thorne had spent the evening phoning every Territo in the telephone book—all fifty-seven—to no avail. By the time he'd finished, he was convinced Cindy had given him a phony name. From there he had no more leads.

Thorne dreaded returning to his office. No doubt there would be enough phone messages to occupy his afternoon—and he was supposed to be working on this merger! He had been placed in charge of an important business deal that meant great things for Oakes-Jenning and for his career. He couldn't let it slide—not when so many others were depending on him. This was not the week to be worrying about Cindy. He had neither the time nor the patience to be running around New York looking for her.

Mrs. Hillard came to a standing position when Thorne entered his office.

"Yes," he barked, and was instantly contrite.

"Mr. Jenning would like to talk to you when you have a spare moment." His secretary's gaze didn't meet his own and Thorne felt a twinge of guilt. He'd been abrupt with her, but it was tame in comparison to his treatment of Sheila. She'd been to see him first thing that morning and he'd hardly been able to look at her as the anger boiled within him. The woman had plotted to ruin his life. It was Sheila's fault that he couldn't locate Cindy. He'd said things to her that he'd never said to anyone. He regretted that now.

Perhaps he might have found it in his heart to forgive her, but she'd revealed no contrition. It almost seemed as if she were proud of what she'd done. He hadn't been the only one to lose his composure. Sheila had called Cindy the most disgusting names. Even now, hours later, Thorne burned with outrage.

In the end, he'd ruthlessly pointed at the door and asked her to leave. Apparently she'd realized her mistake. She began sobbing, ignoring his edict. Gently but firmly, he'd told her he planned to marry Cindy and nothing she could do would change his plans. Then, not knowing what else to do, Thorne had called for his secretary.

"Mrs. Hillard," he'd said, his eyes silently pleading with the older woman for assistance. "It seems Ms. Mathewson needs to powder her nose. Perhaps you could show her the way to the ladies' room."

"Of course."

Mentally Thorne made a note to give his secretary a raise. The older woman had handled the delicate situation with all the finesse of a United Nations ambassador. Tenderly she'd placed her arm around the weeping Sheila's shoulders, and with nothing more than a few whispered words she'd directed her away from Thorne's desk and out of his office.

In his office now, Thorne claimed his chair and unceremoniously looked over the phone messages. Having Paul Jenning ask to see him wasn't a good sign. Unless things went right with this merger, Thorne realized, it could set back his career five years. If only he knew how to contact Cindy....

"Have you been in *his* office yet?"

Cindy had no need to guess whose office Vanessa was referring to. Her co-worker hadn't stopped talking about Thorne from the moment Cindy had arrived for work. "Not yet."

"Will you go in there?"

"Vanessa, it's my job—nothing more and nothing less."

The other girl scooted her cleaning cart down the wide hallway, casting Cindy a worried glance now and then. "How can you be so calm? Aren't you tempted to plant a bomb in his top desk drawer or something?

As far as I'm concerned, Prince is the lowest form of life. He's lower than low. Lower than scum. The pits of all mankind.''

Cindy pressed her lips together and said nothing.

"You're taking this much too calmly."

"What do you want me to do?" Cindy said heatedly; she was quickly losing patience with her fellow worker.

"I don't know," Vanessa returned thoughtfully. "Cry, at least. Weep uncontrollably for a day or two and purge him from your system."

"It would take more than a good bout of crying to do that," Cindy mused. "What else?"

"I don't know what else." Vanessa looked confused. "I'd think you'd want to hate him."

Cindy wasn't allowed that luxury, either. "No, I can't hate him." Not when she loved him more than her very life. Not when she wished for his happiness with every breath she inhaled. Not when everything within her cried with thanksgiving for the short time they'd shared. "No," she repeated softly. "I could never hate him."

They paused outside Thorne's office. "You want me to clean it for you?"

"No." Cindy didn't need to think twice about the offer. From this night forward, this one office would be the only contact she had with Thorne. It was far too much—and not nearly enough.

"You're sure?"

"Positive."

The outer office, which Mrs. Hillard occupied, was neat as always, but Cindy brushed the feather duster over the top of the desk and around the edges of the typewriter. Next, she plugged in the vacuum cleaner.

With a flip of the switch it roared to life, but she hadn't done more than a couple of swipes when it was abruptly switched off. Surprised, Cindy whirled around to discover Thorne holding the plug in his hand.

"Can't this wait?" he stormed, tossing the electric plug onto the carpet. "In case you hadn't noticed, I'm working in here."

Cindy was too stunned to react. It was obvious he hadn't looked at her. She was, after all, only the cleaning woman.

She turned, prepared to leave without another word, but in her rush, she bumped against the side of the desk and knocked over a stack of papers. They fluttered down to the carpet like autumn leaves caught in a gust of wind.

"Of all the, inept, stupid . . ."

Instantly, Cindy crouched down to pick them up, her shaking fingers working as quickly as she could make them cooperate.

"Get out before you do any more damage and I'm forced to fire you."

Cindy reared up, her eyes spitting fire. "How dare you speak to me or anyone else in that demeaning tone," she shouted. She had the satisfaction of watching Thorne's jaw sag open. "You think because you're Mr. Almighty Vice President that you can treat other people like they're your servants? Well, I've got news for you, Thorndike Prince. You can't fire me because—I quit!" With that she removed the feather duster from her hip pocket, shoved it into his hand and stormed out of his office.

Chapter Eleven

Thorne moved quickly, throwing the feather duster aside and hurrying out of his office. So this was Cindy's terrible secret. He had never been more relieved about anything in his life. A flash of pinstriped coveralls and red bandana captured his attention in the office across from his own and he rushed in.

"Cindy, you crazy idiot." He took her by the shoulders, whirled her around and pressed her close to hug the anger out of her.

She struggled, her arms ineffectively flailing right and left, but Thorne wasn't about to set her free. Her cries were muffled against his broad chest.

"Honey, don't fight me. I'm sorry—"

She gasped, braced her palms against him and pushed with all her might until she broke free. If Thorne had been surprised to find Cindy cleaning his office, it was an even greater shock to discover the woman he'd been holding wasn't Cindy.

"I'm not your 'honey,'" Vanessa howled.

"You're not Cindy?"

"Any idiot could see that." Disgruntled, she rearranged her bandana and squared her shoulders. "Do you always behave like an ape-man?"

"Where's Cindy?"

"And you're not exactly the love of my life, either," Vanessa continued sarcastically.

Thorne rushed from the office and down the hall, stopping to search every room. Cindy was gone. Vanished. Frustration came at him like a charging bull. This was the way it happened every time. Just when he thought he'd found her, she disappeared, sending him into agony until she happened to stumble into his life again. No more. They were going to settle this craziness once and for all!

He rushed back to the other girl, braced his hands against the doorway and shouted. "Where'd she go?"

"I don't know that I should tell you." Idly Vanessa dusted the top of Rutherford Hayden's desk, obviously enjoying her moment of glory.

Thorne knotted his fists, growing more impatient by the second. He wasn't going to let this saucy wench keep him from his love. "Either you tell me where she is or you're out of here."

"I wasn't all that keen to keep this job anyway," Vanessa claimed, and faked a yawn.

Thorne was inches from strangling her.

Vanessa sauntered to the other side of the office as though she were a prima donna. "Do you love her?"

"Good Lord, yes!"

"If that's the case, then why was your engagement to another woman printed in the paper?"

"Sheila lied. Now, for God's sake, are you going to tell me where Cindy went?"

"You aren't going to marry this other woman?"

"That's what I just got through telling you. I want to marry Cindy."

Vanessa raised her index finger to her lips, as if giving the weighty matter consideration. "I suppose I *should* tell you, then."

If the woman valued her life, she would do so quickly.

"I was the one who brought Cindy your picture and told her you might be her prince."

"We'll name our first daughter after you," Thorne gritted the words between clenched teeth.

"Fair enough," Vanessa said with a sigh. "Take the elevator all the way to the basement, go to your left, then at the end of the corridor go left again, and it's the first room on your right. Have you got that?"

"Got it." Thorne took off, running. "Left, left, right; left, left, right," he mumbled over and over while he waited for the elevator. The ride to the basement had never seemed more sluggish, especially when he realized that he had to change elevators on the main floor. When he couldn't locate the service elevator, the security guard, Bob Knight, came to his aid.

Just before the heavy door glided shut, Thorne yelled, "We'll name one of our children after you, too!"

Cindy was too furious to think straight. She removed the coveralls and carelessly flung them into the laundry bin. "Can't you see I'm working in here," she muttered, sarcastically mimicking Thorne's words. The red bandana followed the coveralls, falling short of the bin, but Cindy couldn't have cared less.

"Cindy."

At the sound of Thorne calling her name, Cindy turned, closed the door and slid the lock into place.

Thorne tried the door, discovered it was locked, then pounded on it with both fists. "Cindy, I know you're in there!"

She pinched her lips together, refusing to answer him.

"Cindy, for God's sake at least hear me out."

"You don't need to say a word to me, Mr. Almighty Thorndike Prince." Dramatically she placed the back of her wrist to her forehead. "I suggest you leave before you do any more damage and I'm forced to fire you." She taunted him with his own threat.

"Cindy, please, I'm sorry, I had no idea that was you."

She reached for her jeans, sliding them over her hips and snapping them at the waist, her hands shaking in her hurry to dress. "I think you're...despicable. Vanessa was right. You are the lowest of the low."

"She'll have to change her mind. I just promised to name our first daughter after her."

"Oh, stop trying to be clever!"

"Cindy," he tried again, his voice low and coaxing, "hear me out. I've had a rotten day; I was convinced I'd never find you again and one thing after another has gone wrong. You're right, I shouldn't have shouted at you, but please understand, I didn't know you were the cleaning lady."

She rammed her arms into the long sleeves of her JETS sweatshirt and jerked it over her head. "It shouldn't have mattered who I was...you kept telling me that."

"And I meant it. If only you'd let me explain."

"You don't need to explain a thing to me...I'm only the charwoman."

"I love you, charwoman."

He was cheating, telling her that, knowing the effect it would have on her. Undaunted, Cindy threw open the door and faced him, arms akimbo and eyes flashing. "I suppose you love Sheila, too."

"No, I—"

"Don't give me that. Did you think I'm so socially inept, I wouldn't find out about your wedding announcement? I do happen to read the society page now and again."

"Sheila had that printed without my knowledge. I have no intention of ever marrying her. How could I when I'm crazy in love with you?"

That took some of the wind from her sails, and her temper went with it. She closed her eyes and bowed her head. "Don't tell me you love me, Thorne. I don't know that I'll be able to leave you if you do."

Thorne reached for her, astonished anew at how perfectly she fit into his arms and how right it felt to hold her. He held her close and sighed as a great relief moved through him. He had his Cindy, his princess, his love, and he wasn't ever going to release her again.

"That night was all a game," she mumbled. "I never dreamed...never hoped you'd come to care for me."

"The magic never stopped and it never will. You're mine, Cindy Territo."

"But, Thorne, surely you understand now why I couldn't let you know."

"Do you think it matters that you're employed by the janitorial department? I love you. I want you to share my life."

Cindy tensed. "Thorne, I'm frightened."

"There's no reason to be." His hand smoothed the curls at the back of her head in a reassuring motion.

"Are you crazy?" Cindy asked with a sobbing laugh. "Look at us."

Thorne blinked, not understanding.

"You're standing there in your five-hundred-dollar suit and I'm wearing bargain-basement blue jeans."

"So?"

"So! We're like oil and water: we don't mix."

Thorne smiled at that. "It just takes a little shaking up, is all. You can't doubt that we were meant to be together, Cindy, my very own princess."

"But, Thorne..."

He kissed her then, cutting off any further objection. His mouth settled firmly over hers; the kiss was both undeniably gentle and magically sweet. When he held her like this it was so easy to believe everything would always be this wonderful between them.

"I want to meet your family."

"Thorne, no." Cindy broke out of his arms, hugging her waist.

He looked stunned. "Why not?"

"Because—"

"I'll need to meet them sometime."

Her Uncle Sal's contorted, angry face flashed before Cindy. She knew he strongly disapproved of Thorne. If Cindy were to bring Thorne to the apartment, Sal would punch first and ask questions later. Any one of her uncles would behave the same way. Her family was highly protective of all their loved ones, and there would need to be a whole lot of explaining done before Cindy brought Thorne into their midst.

"Meet them?" Cindy repeated. "Why?"

"Cindy." He held her squarely by the shoulders. "I plan to marry you."

She blinked twice, overwhelmed with a flood of happiness and then immediately swamped with the backwash of doubts.

"You will be my wife, won't you?"

He asked with such tenderness that Cindy's eyes brimmed with tears. She bit her bottom lip and shook her head. "Yes..."

Thorne relaxed.

"No," she said quickly, then covered her face with both hands. "Oh, good grief, I don't know!"

"Do you love me?"

Her response was a vigorous nod.

"Then it's settled." He removed her hands from her face and kissed her eyes and her nose. Unable to stop, his lips descended slowly toward her mouth, nibbling along the way, pausing at her earlobe, working their way across the delicate line of her jaw....

"But, Thorne, nothing's settled. Not really. We...I need time."

"Okay, I'll give you time."

The organ music vibrated through the church. Cindy stood at the back of St. Anthony's and her heart went still as the first bridesmaid, holding a large bouquet of pink rosebuds, stepped forward. The second and the third followed. Cindy watched their progress, and her heart throbbed with happiness. This was her wedding day and within the hour she would experience the birth of her dreams. She would become Thorne's wife. Somehow they'd crossed every hurdle. She'd claimed she needed time. He'd given it to her. She was convinced her family would object, but with gentle patience Thorne had won over every member. Now it was June and almost six months had passed since the night of the Christmas Ball. Thorne had convinced her the magic of that night would last all through their lives, and finally Cindy could believe him. She hadn't thought it was possible to love anyone as much as she loved Thorne. There wasn't anything in this world their love couldn't overcome. They'd proved it.

Confident, Thorne stood at the altar, waiting for her. His eyes were filled with such a wondrous glow of tenderness that Cindy was forced to resist the urge to race into his arms.

His smile lent her assurance. He didn't look the least bit nervous, while Cindy felt as if a squad of bombers were about to invade her stomach. From the first, he'd been the confident one. Always so sure of what was right for them. Never doubting. Oh, dear Lord, how she loved him.

The signal for four-year-old Carla to join the procession came, and dressed in her long lavender gown, the little girl took one measured step after another.

Cindy stood at the back of the church and looked out over the seated guests. To her left were those who had loved and nurtured her most of her life. Her Aunt Theresa sat in the front row, a lace handkerchief clenched in her hand, and Cindy saw her dab away an escaped tear of happiness. Cousins abounded. Aunts, uncles, lifelong friends, Vanessa, Bob Knight and others who had come to share this glorious day of joy.

To her right was Thorne's family. Wealthy, cultured, sophisticated. St. Anthony's parking lot had never housed so many Cadillacs and Mercedes, nor had this humble sanctuary witnessed so many fur coats and expensive suits. But they'd come, filling the large church to capacity, wanting to meet the woman who was about to become Thorne's wife.

The organ music reached a climax of sound when Cindy stepped onto the trail of white linen that ran the length of the wide aisle. The train of the satin and lace dress that had been worn by both her mother and her aunt flowed behind her. The adrenaline pumped through Cindy's blood as she moved, each resounding note of the organ drawing her closer to Thorne, her prince, her love.

The congregation stood and Cindy experienced a throb of excitement as the faces of those she loved turned to watch her progress.

Thirty minutes later Cindy moved back down the same aisle as Thorne's wife. Family and friends spilled out of the church, crowding the steps. Cindy was repeatedly hugged and Thorne shook hand after hand.

The limousine arrived, and with his guiding hand at her elbow, Thorne led her down the steps and held open the car door for her.

Almost immediately, he climbed in after her.

"Hello, Mrs. Prince," he whispered, his voice filled with awe. "Have I told you today how much I love you?" he asked, and his eyes contained a tender glow.

"You just did that with a church full of witnesses," she reminded him softly. "I do love you, Thorne. There were so many times I didn't believe this day could ever happen, and now that it has, I know how right it is."

He gathered her in his arms and kissed her to the boisterous approval of their guests, who were still watching from the sidewalk.

"Did you see the banner?" Thorne asked, pointing to the outside of the church.

"No."

"I think Vanessa and the company had something to do with that."

Cindy laughed. There, above three double-width doors a banner was hung, the words bold and bright for all the world to read: CINDY AND HER PRINCE LIVED HAPPILY EVER AFTER.

* * * * *

*Look for SOME KIND OF WONDERFUL,
BOOK II in Debbie Macomber's
LEGENDARY LOVERS TRILOGY, available
in March from Silhouette Romance.
Don't miss it!*

READERS' COMMENTS ON SILHOUETTE ROMANCES:

"The best time of my day is when I put my children to bed at naptime and sit down to read a Silhouette Romance. Keep up the good work."

P.M.*, Allegan, MI

"I am very fond of the quality of your Silhouette Romances. They are so real. I have tried to read some of the other romances, but I always come back to Silhouette."

C.S., Mechanicsburg, PA

"I feel that Silhouette Books offer a wider choice and/or variety than any of the other romance books available."

R.R., Aberdeen, WA

"I have enjoyed reading Silhouette Romances for many years now. They are light and refreshing. You can always put yourself in the main characters' place, feeling alive and beautiful."

J.M.K., San Antonio, TX

"My boyfriend always teases me about Silhouette Books. He asks me, how's my love life and naturally I say terrific, but I tell him that there is always room for a little more romance from Silhouette."

F.N., Ontario, Canada

*names available on request

Silhouette ❤ *Romance*

COMING NEXT MONTH

#556 NEVER LOVE A COWBOY—Rita Rainville
Anne Sheldon thought she was resigned to widowhood and could live off her happy memories, but Ben Benedict knew better. He was sure Anne deserved a future as well as a past—a future that included him.

#557 DONOVAN'S MERMAID—Helen R. Myers
Chief of police Sam Donovan was Gulls Drift's most confirmed bachelor until he rescued Miranda Paley from the Gulf of Mexico. Now Sam's heart needed rescuing from Randi's captivating smile. Would the little town of Gulls Drift ever be the same?

#558 A KISS IS STILL A KISS—Colleen Christie
Kurt Lawrence needed feisty Margo Shepherd to help him revamp his video chain. But after an impulsive kiss and a case of mistaken identity, how could he assure her he was strictly business? Especially when the memory of her lips had him longing to mix business with pleasure....

#559 UNDER A DESERT SKY—Arlene James
Jamie Goff had been born in the Nevada desert, and her heart had always belonged under an endless sky. But when citified Bronson Taylor laid claim to her love, Jamie was torn—Bron must return to the city. Would Jamie have to choose between her two loves?

#560 THE OUTSIDER—Stella Bagwell
Luke Chandler had arrived just in the nick of time to save Faith Galloway's ranch, but Faith felt more than gratitude for her mysterious new employee. Was Faith's love strong enough to convince the handsome drifter that it was time to settle down?

#561 WIFE WANTED—Terri Herrington
Tycoon Joe Dillon had launched the perfect advertising campaign to find himself a wife, but the woman he wanted hadn't applied for the job. He'd have to do some powerful persuading to show "happily single" Brit Alexander that the man behind the slogans had a heart of gold....

AVAILABLE THIS MONTH:

Silhouette Romance™

Legendary Lovers Trilogy

BY DEBBIE MACOMBER....

ONCE UPON A TIME, in a land not so far away, there lived a girl, Debbie Macomber, who grew up dreaming of castles, white knights and princes on fiery steeds. Her family was an ordinary one with a mother and father and one wicked brother, who sold copies of her diary to all the boys in her junior high class.

One day, when Debbie was only nineteen, a handsome electrician drove by in a shiny black convertible. Now Debbie knew a prince when she saw one, and before long they lived in a two-bedroom cottage surrounded by a white picket fence.

As often happens when a damsel fair meets her prince charming, children followed, and soon the two-bedroom cottage became a four-bedroom castle. The kingdom flourished and prospered, and between soccer games and car pools, ballet classes and clarinet lessons, Debbie thought about love and enchantment and the magic of romance.

One day Debbie said, "What this country needs is a good fairy tale." She remembered how well her diary had sold and she dreamed again of castles, white knights and princes on fiery steeds. And so the stories of Cinderella, Beauty and the Beast, and Snow White were reborn....

Look for Debbie Macomber's *Legendary Lovers* trilogy from Silhouette Romance: *Cindy and the Prince* (January, 1988); *Some Kind of Wonderful* (March, 1988); *Almost Paradise* (May, 1988). Don't miss them!

SRT-1